The Alpha's Mate
Huntsville Pack Book 1

Michelle Fox

DEDICATION

With love to my readers!

Michelle Fox
For the love of fangs and fur

Other Books in the Huntsville Series

Bring Her Wolf ~ FREE!

The Alpha's Mate ~ 4.5 stars from Night Owl Reviews.

The Alpha's Justice ~ 5 fangs from Paranormal Romance Junkies.

The Alpha's Fight

More by Michelle Fox

First Moon ~ 5 stars from Night Owl Reviews

Moon's Law ~ 5 stars from Night Owl Reviews

BLURB

Little known fact about being a werewolf: There are always wolves at your door and some of them are up to no good.

Chloe Weiss' dreams have finally come true: She's a null no more, her wolf has finally come. She's now a full member of her pack in the remote Appalachian 'were town' of Huntsville. Even better, she's mated to the pack's next alpha, Jackson Swift. However, now that she's on the other side of her happy ending, things aren't quite as rosy as she'd expected.

The women of her pack resent her status as alpha's mate and suddenly there are rumors that Chloe is an Omega, a werewolf so weak they are banned from ever mating. Worse, an old friend of Jackson's blows into town full of disapproval....and competition. It seems no one likes Chloe except Jackson.

Then women start disappearing, violently kidnapped from their homes and never heard from again. There's a killer on the loose in the small town of Huntsville, and the one wolf he'd do anything to have is Chloe.

Now Chloe will have to fight...for Jackson, her place in the pack, and her life.

1

"I think my wolf hates me." I rolled over in bed and snuggled up against Jackson with a pout. It had been two weeks since he brought my wolf and claimed me as his mate. My life should be perfect. I had everything I ever wanted; a place in the pack and my very own 'tall, dark and handsome' man to warm my bed, but things weren't seamless.

I felt itchy in my new skin, as if it wasn't the right size. From the way some of the other wolves treated me, it seemed they felt the same. I hadn't fit in when everyone thought I was a null and now I didn't fit in as a wolf.

Jackson wrapped a strong arm around me and gave me a reassuring squeeze. "It just takes some time, Clo. Changing is awkward at first."

"She looks at me like I'm offending her." I frowned. She was doing it right now, in fact. Whenever I blinked, her haughty expression flashed against the backs of my eyelids. "How does your wolf look at *you*?"

He cocked his head and thought for a moment. "He just looks at me."

"That's it?" I sighed and rolled away. Jackson oozed sex like a pagan god and he looked the part too, with his sculpted muscles, dark molten chocolate eyes, and black, wavy hair. However, it sometimes seemed he didn't think overmuch about anything but sex. Not that I was complaining. He was a fantastic lover, but I would've appreciated a little introspection just then. Maybe all the hot steamy sex we had was messing with the blood supply to his brain.

Punching my pillow, I attempted to settle in for the night. Sleep eluded me more often than not these days. Every time I closed my eyes, there was my wolf, her gleaming yellow gaze boring into my brain. She seemed to be expecting or wanting something, but I had no idea what.

"I know a way to guarantee sweet dreams." Jackson's hand spun little circles on my shoulder as his other hand inched the covers off me. I shivered, both from his touch and the cool air. We'd started our relationship in the fall when the sun was still strong enough to blunt the chill. Now, on the cusp of winter, the air nipped at my skin.

"Oh really?" I arched an eyebrow and resisted the urge to pull the covers back over me. Jackson was warmer anyway. Not to mention he provided orgasms.

"Yep." He straddled my hips and leaned down to nuzzle the nape of my neck.

"Let me guess." I put a finger to my lips and pretended to think very hard. "Is it *sex*?"

His deep chuckle seemed to rumble through my body as well as his. "Yep." Jackson gently kissed my neck working his way to the hollow of my throat.

"Again?" I gave a soft gasp as his lips roamed my sensitive flesh. We went at it so often I wondered if we were really rabbits. The sensual pull between us was magnetic. We almost couldn't help ourselves.

"And again," he murmured in a baritone so deep, it vibrated through my neck. "I can't get enough of you Chloe. Not since the day I first saw you."

I laughed. I couldn't help it. "That's why you slept with every other bitch in the pack, right?"

He sighed, but knew I wasn't truly angry. Before we'd clarified things between us, he'd tried to find someone else to claims as his. Cal, our alpha, had put a lot of pressure on Jackson to mate and cement his relationship with the pack. Jackson wasn't just new to the Huntsville pack, Cal planned for my alpha lover to take his place when the time came, which meant he needed a mate.

As a result, he'd told Jackson to avoid me because I was a null--I would never be a true wolf let alone an alpha's mate. So, trying to find a match, Jackson slept with every bitch who'd shown interest. Sometimes two different ones on the same night. By the time he brought my wolf and claimed me, he'd slept with almost every eligible female in the pack.

We'd fought about his many flings at first, but I no longer carried any bitterness. Jackson was mine. I was his. There was no going back. That didn't mean, though, that I wouldn't give him shit about it.

The only problem? He gave me shit right back.

He paused, just on the threshold of entering me and stared into my eyes. "Mine," he growled.

I nodded and arched my pelvis, reaching for him. "Yours." I'd been uncertain when he first claimed me and sometimes still struggled with the idea of being half of an instant power couple. Back when I couldn't change, I'd been a zero and no one paid much attention to me. Mating with Jackson would someday make me the alpha female of the pack. When I was alone with Jackson we fit perfectly, but, outside our bedroom, we barely knew each other.

Jackson slammed into me, bringing my focus to heel. I watched his face above me. He had the strong, sculpted features of a movie star and I never tired of looking at him. He watched me too, his hands still around my wrists pinning me tight. I twisted in his grip wanting to touch him, but he didn't budge. While I was stronger than ever since the change, I still couldn't top an alpha like Jackson.

"Let me go," I panted.

"I like you this way." He smiled and dipped his head to suck my nipple. "You're mine to fuck senseless."

"Oh God," I hissed arching up toward his mouth.

He laughed, a strong rumble that vibrated through his mouth to my nipple. I whimpered when he began swirling his tongue over and over the taut nub of my breast. His cock continued to plunge my slick depths and my nipples grew tighter and tighter, feeding the aching pleasure at my core.

"I'm going to come," I said.

"Yes, do it. Come for me, she-wolf." He thrust into me even harder and that sent me over the edge. The orgasm shook me like a seizure. I couldn't talk or think, let alone breathe. A series of big and small explosions detonated in my nervous system, and, if Jackson hadn't been there to physically hold me together, I would've blown apart. I was sure of it.

When I could function again, Jackson remained hard inside me. I knew what that meant. He was holding back because he wasn't done with me yet. The man had exquisite control and loved to coax multiple orgasms from me.

"I love watching you come," he said.

"You love *making* me come," I corrected.

He nodded. "That too. In fact, I'd like to go for another round."

My body quickened with excitement at his words while my wolf howled in happy assent. Then I caught sight of the bedside clock, which informed me it was two a.m.

"I have to be up at six," I said in weak protest. I was supposed to drive to Nashville to go look at wedding dresses. Wolves love a good wedding, and, given Jackson's future as pack alpha, we couldn't call ourselves mated and stop there. No, we had to have a wedding with all the trimmings. A good old fashioned mating jamboree. I was alternately terrified and excited at the prospect.

"I'm up *now*." Jackson pulled out of me and then slowly inched his way back inside to make his point.

I groaned as he filled me back up. Who was I kidding? I would stay up all night to fuck him and love it. He made me feel whole. I'd been lonely, so very lonely before Jackson came into my life. My parents died years ago, leaving me alone in a pack I couldn't join. Jackson had changed everything.

"Sleep is for the weak." I squeezed his length, allowing my body the pleasure of tracing the outline of his cock.

"Damn right." He yanked on my hands and pulled me upright, until we sat facing each other.

"Oh," I said with a shudder. The change in position caused my breasts to rub across his chest as we moved against each other. His cock delved deeper than before, splitting my core wide and exposing its sensitive center.

"There, that's more comfortable." Jackson kissed me, one hand going to cradle the back of my head.

"Mmm," I murmured my agreement, my mouth too occupied to allow me to form actual words. He had this glorious way of nipping at my lips and then slurping the entire bottom one into his mouth. It made me weak in the knees every time.

Another bonus of our position change, my hands were now

free and I let them roam his body. His muscles flowed in subtle hills and valleys. I travelled them all with lingering caresses. No other bitch would touch him again. This was my right now and mine alone.

Cupping his face in my hands, I took control of our kisses. "Mine," I said and then I bit down on his lower lip.

Jackson growled at me and I bit harder. My hips circled faster, riding him rough and hard. He reached a hand down to where we were joined, slipping a finger between my lips to stroke the sensitive nub there.

My jaw went slack as I gasped and he took the opportunity to bite my lip the same way I'd bitten his. His teeth pricked my skin like sharp little knives and his finger toyed with me, pushing me closer to another release. Goosebumps skittered over my skin. Everything was too tight now; my nipples, my skin, even my wet passage, which wrapped itself around him and squeezed like a python.

"Jackson," I said, almost crying. Behind my eyelids, my wolf began to howl.

"Are you going to come for me again, my little she-wolf?" He thrust his hips at me, meeting mine.

"Oh, yes." I could only shriek as the orgasm washed over me.

This time Jackson couldn't hold out, I was squeezing him too hard. His body quivered against mine and his hard shaft jerked inside me as he came.

He buried his head in my neck. "Chloe," he said almost forlornly.

"Yes, Jackson?" I collapsed into him. We wrapped our arms around each other and a deep contentment filled the air between us. Behind my eyelids, I saw that we mirrored the way our wolves had collapsed into each other. His dark sable wolf wrapped himself almost all the way around my wolf, contrasting with her coppery brown coat. He was large enough to be scary, but I felt no fear. I liked the way he filled me up and took up the space around me. It made me feel safe, and, not just loved, but wanted. Something I hadn't experienced before.

"Mine," was all he said, hands fisting in my hair.

I rubbed his back. "Yours. And you are mine too."

"Yes," he said pulling me down to lie beside him. "Always."

"Forever," I added. The idea both thrilled and scared me senseless. I'd lost everything before and now that I had everything, I felt like it would be torn away from me once again. I didn't know if I could survive that loss a second time.

We fell asleep in a tangle of limbs, pressed so close together that we could feel each other's heart beats.

2

You'd think that werewolves would lead lives of action and adventure, using their superior strength and senses to their advantage.

You would be wrong.

In reality, wolves like to overeat (mostly chicken wings) and gossip. They especially love a good rumor, the more scandalous, the more salacious, the better. I knew firsthand how insular packs could be as I'd been the subject of wagging tongues my whole life. Being the only null in four generations could do that to you.

Except there was one rumor no one had ever heard and it was true: I'd never actually been a null. I'd just been delayed. A true null never would've shifted. The real mystery was what had kept my wolf at bay for so long. I suspected it was related to my parents' deaths. If that didn't set a wolf back, I didn't know what would.

Now that I'd finally changed and mated with Jackson, the scrutiny approached the intensity of a super nova. *Everyone* talked about me. *All* the time. They'd spent my whole life ignoring me, pushing me to the fringes of the pack and now they couldn't stop noticing me. I was the biggest news to break in the small Appalachian town of Hunstville in decades.

The next alpha female of the Huntsville pack would be me, the 'null' who couldn't change until her mate brought her wolf. The gossip ranged from claiming I was deformed to mentally unstable. To escape speculation, I'd taken to hiding in the house I now shared with Jackson.

Being the center of attention made me anxious. I had few friends and still didn't quite trust my instincts as a wolf. Because I'd been shunned by the pack so long, I barely knew how a pack was even supposed to work. It was safer to keep to myself. I lived in fear of letting anyone see me struggle with my transition to a full werewolf. It would look like weakness instead of inexperience and there were wolves who would be more than happy to see me fail.

Today, however, I couldn't stay out of the public eye. There was a package waiting for me at the post office and I wanted to pick it up before I ran down to Nashville. Jackson was gone when I woke up, already over at Cal's house on pack business. Something about renegotiating mineral rights with the mining company that leased some of the pack's land.

Being a generally thoughtful guy, he made enough coffee for both of us before he left. I sipped it as I drove toward town, enjoying the hazelnut flavor.

I parked my Toyota pick-up—so ancient the cherry red had long ago faded to pink—as near to the post office as I could and checked my cell phone for the time. My truck's clock stopped working sometime in the 1990s, back when my Dad was still alive.

It was Saturday, the busiest day of the week for our small town square. I'd hoped to avoid notice by being there when the post office opened at seven. The original idea had been to get in and get out before anyone saw me. Unfortunately, my cell phone showed the time as five after eleven. Jackson had kept me up so late, I'd sank back into sleep instead of getting up when the alarm went off. Naturally, that meant post office was packed. So much for my plan to stay on the down low.

Squaring my shoulders, I stepped out of my truck, and after a brief moment of hesitation, opened the squeaky door to the post office. Bells clinked against the glass door announcing my arrival to everyone inside. I tried not to cringe at the sound. Blinking against the dim light, I took my place in line, acting like it was no big deal when, in reality, I hadn't been around so many people in weeks.

One or two folks nodded at me in polite acknowledgement and I nodded back, noting the ones who turned up their noses, pretending I was invisible. As usual, it was the younger wolves who seemed to be the most offended by my existence. The older ones were more accepting of my sudden transformation and elevation in the pack's hierarchy.

The varied scents of everyone waiting with me hit my nose,

all carrying the distinctive tang of a werewolf. Only wolves lived in Huntsville and we didn't need much in terms of human comforts. We had a bar, a grocery store, a bakery, a school, a gas station and a post office. An old brick Victorian mansion served as City Hall, housing what little government we needed to get by in a largely human world. The expansive house had been built by Heinrich Schmidt, a German wolf fleeing World War I. He brought his pack here and we'd prospered ever since.

I often wondered what he would think about me. Not every pack drove out its nulls, but Heinrich had apparently been influenced by Nazi racial purity doctrine: If you couldn't shift, you had to go.

Thankfully, future generations were a little more lenient. Cal, our current pack alpha, had let me stay as long as he could. If not for his leniency, I would've been long gone before Jackson ever came to town.

We kept Huntsville tiny on purpose. Humans weren't welcome and we stayed off their radar by looking too small to bother with. Anything that couldn't be found in town, we ordered online. Or, if absolutely necessary, we could drive the thirty minutes into Hudson which boasted a small mall. Nashville was just a couple hours away as well and we sometimes shopped there.

I transferred my weight from foot to foot as I waited in line and watched as Jana Schwartz, the post mistress, beckoned people forward. Fine lines crisscrossed her weathered face and she had a stout, grandmotherly figure. I didn't know her well, but appreciated her prompt efficiency in dispatching customers at a rapid pace. Jana wasn't wasting any time and it seemed she didn't like having a line as much as no one wanted to be in one.

Behind me, I heard the squeak of rusty hinges and the jangle of bells as the door opened, ushering in multiple footsteps. I turned to see Vicki Richter along with her usual entourage of cronies join the line.

The tall brunette and I weren't friends, but we'd never been enemies either. When my wolf came, though, I somehow became her mortal enemy overnight.

Of all the women Jackson slept with, she'd taken their fling the most seriously. She'd been harassing me every chance she got and I doubted today would be any different.

Within seconds, the whispering started, quickly filling the cramped quarters of the post office. The building dated back to the thirties and felt tight with three people. At the moment, almost a dozen of us were squeezed inside, the gossip filling what little space there was between us. It was impossible not to overhear.

I kept my eyes forward, but I knew the voices badmouthing me well. My heart pounded in my chest as I realized I was trapped.

"She was a null," said Alan, a gangly beta wolf with an overbite. He'd been mooning after Vicki for years. Did he not realize he was the means to an end named Jackson? Vicki would never take up with him, not in a million years.

"Somehow he got her to change," Tony said, the low bass tenor of his voice was unmistakable. I didn't know him well, but he liked to wear leather with metal spikes and hang around Vicki, which pretty much told me everything I needed to know.

"She looks like a null. Are you sure she's shifted?" came a high, sweet voice I didn't recognize. I peeked over my shoulder to see a young girl—no doubt, newly changed—standing with them, her narrow face full of disgust. Great, Vicki was spreading her hate of me, infecting everyone she could find. Including small children who'd barely sprouted their first fur.

"And now she's mated to Jackson, can you believe it?" This was Vicki, her disapproval emanating from her in waves of sour scent. She smelled like bad meat, like something you would never put in your mouth. It was hard to believe she was a gorgeous dark haired, blue-eyed beauty. Maybe if Jackson had let his nose lead, he would've steered clear of her in the first place. As my mom always used to say, 'you're only as pretty as you smell.'

"She don't look like much." John's voice carried so much disgust, I winced.

The scent of werewolf now mixed with a foulness that accompanied negative emotions. Anger surged through me, thundering in my ears like a war drum. I whirled around and met Vicki's stormy blue eyes, staring her down. When she boldly held my gaze, refusing to look away, my wolf's power bristled over my skin.

She remained unimpressed and looked just as pissed as I was. Her lips curled, baring her very sharp canines outlined with red lipstick.

"You have a problem with me?" My voice came out in a snarl as it entered the vocal range of a wolf.

She crossed her arms and tossed her head, flinging her dark hair out of her face. "Well, *duh.*"

I stepped closer to her until we almost touched. "Watch yourself." My tolerance snapped and my temper flared hotter than lighter fluid on coals. I was so done with Vicki and her digs. It was time to lay down the law.

"Or what?" She lifted her chin in a haughty gesture.

Without thinking, I wrapped a hand around her neck. We were about the same size and my hand shouldn't have been able to span her throat, but it did. With shock, I realized my bones had lengthened, until my hand was big enough. I wasn't shifting; my wolf form matched my human size, putting me more on the petite end of the spectrum. This was something else, something new. Jackson told me I would come into my full wolf powers gradually and here was proof.

I'd surprised Vicki, too. She tried not to show it, but her pupils dilated. Her scent changed subtly as well, emitting the tart scent of fear. I squeezed and the fear stink grew strong as a skunk. Alan, Tony and John covered their noses and backed away, refusing to meet my eyes or Vicki's.

Someone behind me said, "Is she going to kill her?"

The question brought me back to my senses. At least a little. Enough that I peeled my hand away from her throat and let her go.

"No, I'm not going to kill her," I said more to reassure myself than anyone else. Rage still ran hot in me and screamed for an outlet, preferably one that included ramming Vicki's head into the nearest wall.

Vicki coughed and rubbed her throat. "She couldn't kill me even if she wanted to."

Vicki's persistence made me blink. I'd almost popped her head like a pimple and yet she continued to provoke me. Amazing.

"Don't make me regret letting you go," I said with dangerous calm. My wolf growled in my mind's eye and pawed at the ground, desperate to leap out and finish what I'd almost started. It took everything I had to maintain control.

"You're weak, bitch. Too weak to be an alpha's mate. Right?" She looked to the guys who nodded, tentative at first, but then with increasing confidence.

"Yeah. She's an Omega," Alan said. "She shouldn't be mated with Jackson."

The word Omega gave me pause. They were weak wolves and most packs refused to let them mate, not wanting their weakness to taint pack bloodlines. Back when everyone thought I was a null, I'd been something lower than even an Omega. It was the equivalent of being born blind, deaf and dumb in the human world. At least Omega wolves could still change, even if they were scrawny and sickly.

Sometimes packs killed them outright, preferring to exterminate weak genetics altogether. It wouldn't surprise me if

Vicki's sentiments on the issue ran toward the more extreme end of the spectrum.

"Vicki?" I said.

"Yeah," she looked at me, her confidence back at full throttle. All of her earlier fear had vanished, and in its place, I smelled a cloying self-satisfaction.

"I'm not an Omega." I advanced on her again, forcing her to step back and give ground to my dominance.

"Yeah, you are." She looked up and down, her upper lip curled in disgust. "You've always been nothing, Chloe. Just because you can shift now doesn't change that and I'm not the only one who's noticed."

I wanted to roll my eyes, but kept them narrowed on Vicki. "Don't you get it?" I shook my head, deciding to speak plainly. No doubt the unvarnished truth would hurt, but maybe it would get her to move on. "Jackson couldn't choose you even if he wanted to. You're not his mate, Vicki. Not now, not ever. I'm not your competition because there isn't one. You were a mistake, one that Jackson won't repeat."

She lunged for me, hands flailing and nails morphing into claws as she did so. I stepped to the side and then caught her by the throat again. The speed with which I moved startled me. I was getting faster. I lifted her up by the throat, unsure if I could do it until I actually did it.

I smiled in triumph. I was stronger, too. Giving her a little shake, I said. "Let it go, Vicki. Move on before you really get hurt.

Live to find your true mate." I dropped her then and she fell to the floor with a growl.

Jumping to her feet with a light footed grace, she said, "I'm not letting this go, bitch. You're an Omega. You don't even deserve to live." Vicki stabbed the air with a sharp nailed finger.

I sighed. "Mark my words, next time I get a hand around your neck, I won't stop squeezing." If she ignored that warning, I wouldn't hold back next time. She'd been following me around since I'd mated with Jackson, calling me names and generally being nasty. I was done with it. If she wanted to escalate things, I wouldn't turn her away. Not anymore.

She gave a harsh laugh. "Next time I see you, bitch, you'll be in the pack clearing failing the test of blood. We'll tear you limb from limb and howl with glee as we do it."

Tossing her head, she turned on her heel and left the post office, her groupies trailing behind like eager puppies. A tense silence hung in the air at their departure. No one looked at anyone, which was how wolves avoided conflict. We all cast our gazes upward as if the ceiling held a mural painted by Michelangelo as opposed to its more mundane flat white paint turned gray with age. At the same time, you could bet everyone's ears were perked, waiting to hear my reaction.

Behind the counter, Jana heaved a sigh and said, "Next, please."

With that, an uneasy normalcy resumed in the post office. We shuffled forward in line, picking up and dropping off packages.

Jana beckoned me forward with a kind smile when my turn came.

I handed her the card the mailman had left in our mailbox. "I have a package."

She nodded. "Yes, all the way from Ireland too."

Jana bent over, rummaging around under the counter and when she straightened back up, she held a small box in her hand. White and red 'fragile' stickers adorned its side.

"Sign here." She set the box aside and pointed to a signature line on the package notification.

I grabbed the pen chained to the counter and quickly scrawled my signature.

Looking at the card, she said, "That was good, Chloe."

"It was?" I asked, confused. In school, my teachers had always taken off points for penmanship. I didn't think my signature was good enough to warrant compliments.

"I meant with Vicki. The alpha's mate has to be strong. Don't let bullies like her push you around. If she's dumb enough to call the test of blood, she'll be the one torn apart, not you."

"Oh, thanks," I mumbled. I appreciated Jana's support, especially since I really didn't know what I was doing. I'd gone on instinct in the post office, hoping I didn't do anything really stupid. I didn't even actually know what the test of blood was, but I wasn't about to admit that in public. I would ask Jackson about it later.

She waved me forward, leaning over the counter to quietly say, "I remember when Cal took his mate. It wasn't much easier for her, but she got through it in the end."

"Really?" I couldn't keep the surprise from my voice. I would always remember Cal's wife as a woman no one ignored. Everyone had listened to Betty without question.

Jana nodded. "Give it time. The pack has to know they can trust you and they'll test you until they're sure."

I blinked as her words sank in. I hadn't thought of it like that. Maybe all this friction was normal, part and parcel of being the alpha's mate. If so, I needed to toughen up and fast. "Thanks, Jana." I smiled at her, grateful for her kindness.

She smiled back. "Any time."

Taking my package, I hustled out of the post office, keenly aware of all the eyes watching me go. Now that the tension of my confrontation with Vicki had dissipated, they, apparently, felt free to openly stare at me. The gossip I'd provided that morning would fuel them like caffeine, their jaws flapping non-stop as they recounted the latest exploits of the alpha's ill-chosen mate. It made me want to crawl into a deep, dark hole and never come out again.

I silently cursed companies that required a signature for their deliveries. Yes, the crystal champagne flutes I'd ordered were very expensive and fragile, but the much more expensive wedding band for Jackson had been left on my porch no problem. From here on out, I vowed to only work with companies that wouldn't force me into town to pick up their goods.

Frowning about my mail problems, I blinked as the sun's brilliance hit my eyes. The day was cloudless and cold. The generously late Indian summer had faded over a week ago, and it now appeared the weather was fixing to grace us with the first snow of the season. I dropped the package off in my truck and then headed to the bar, wanting to order something to eat before I undertook the drive to Nashville.

I was just about to open the door and step inside when the loud squeal of tires made me pause. Looking over my shoulder, I saw a red corvette roaring down the street. Frowning, I let the door to the bar go and stepped back onto the sidewalk.

No one in Huntsville drove a sports car. We were pick-up truck people. Fancy cars were beyond our pay grade. We weren't poor by any means, but our economics were limited to working in town or helping to administer the pack land.

We owned over five hundred acres, most of which was reserved for us to run. The edge of our property housed cabins that we rented out to the public. We also leased the mineral rights to a big mining company. They operated a coal mine in a gulley that was too steep for us to access in wolf form. The pack split the profits, which made for a comfortable existence, but not an extravagant one.

As I watched, the corvette zoomed through the town square and then jackknifed into a parking spot right in front of me. I held my breath, expecting the car to jump the curb and hit me, but the driver exercised the precision of a professional and the vehicle shrieked to a stop just before hitting the curb.

The noise attracted notice. Anyone outside stopped same as I had, riveted by the corvette's progression. The car purred, the sound anything but content, and then the driver turned it off. The sudden silence rang in the air like an alarm bell.

I waited, curious to see who the driver was and ready to direct the stranger to Hudson, the nearest human city about twenty miles down the road. We weren't so barbaric as to run humans out of town, but, if they insisted on eating at the bar, the service would be terrible and the food either undercooked or burnt. No one came back twice if they could help it. Not unless they belonged.

To my surprise, the driver who emerged from the corvette's interior, was a woman. Given the crazy driving, I'd expected a young, cocky guy. Instead, a striking redhead stepped out of the car, sharp stilettos clacking on the concrete.

She stood tall as a super model and svelte as one, too. Her red wrap dress and designer stilettos spoke of money and her scent identified her as a wolf, just not one from Huntsville. Checking out the front plate, I noted she was from Louisiana.

Funnily enough, so was Jackson.

Lifting her sunglasses to the top of her head, she quickly scanned the area with bright green eyes. Zeroing in on me, she sniffed and said, "Are you the bitch who thinks she can have my mate?"

Her voice carried in the quiet pre-winter air to the point where people inside the bar came out to better hear her. Wolves can smell anything, especially good gossip fodder.

3

"Excuse me?" I asked, utterly confused.

She stalked toward me and leaned down until we were eye-to-eye, the gesture making me feel very short and very fat in comparison. She narrowed her eyes into emerald slits and repeated her question. "I said, are you the bitch who thinks she can have my mate?"

"Your mate being?" I asked, although I had a sinking feeling who it was.

"Jackson Swift," she said with a tight smile that showed off her sharp, pointy canine teeth.

"Kelsey," came Jackson's voice before I could respond. We both turned to see him coming down the sidewalk, a wide-eyed look of surprise on his face.

He greeted her with a warm hug. "What are you doing here?"

Kelsey laughed and the trilling sound made my hackles rise. "Just checking up on you." She looped her arm through

Jackson's and looked at me. "Making sure this town is doing right by my best friend."

Seeing the confusion on my face, she smiled at me. "Sorry, um, Chloe is it? I was just having some fun with you. Jackson's mom showed me a picture, and, when I saw you, I just couldn't resist the temptation to pull your leg."

I pushed out a fake chuckle while giving Jackson a 'WTF' look. Seriously. *What. The. Fuck?* "You didn't tell me she was coming."

He shrugged and gave me an equally 'WTF' look. "I had no idea."

"I swore your mom to secrecy. You know she can't tell me no." She snuggled up to Jackson, which made me want to rip her face off.

My hands curled into fists, the nails breaking the skin of my palms. "What are you doing here?" I cleared my throat several times as I spoke to keep my voice from coming out in a hostile growl. My wolf was practically frothing with anger. Vicki had already put her on edge and now Kelsey threatened to push us both over. If I wasn't careful, I would shift right here, right now and it would be a blood bath. The arch look Kelsey gave me suggested she knew exactly what effect her appearance had on me.

"I'm an event planner on the side and when I heard Jackson was hitched, I thought I'd come help out with the wedding." She scanned the town, taking in the few paint worn buildings lining the street and wrinkled her nose. "You know, help you make it an event to remember. The Swift pack likes to celebrate with class."

Jackson smiled at me weakly. "How about we grab a bite to eat, ladies?"

So we all traipsed into the bar, Kelsey laughing lightly as if she didn't have a care in the world and constantly touching Jackson. For his part, Jackson looked happy to see her although from the concerned looks he shot my way, he seemed to have picked up on the fact that I wasn't as thrilled. I trailed behind them glowering and fighting the urge to start a bar brawl. The entire bar fell silent, acutely aware of our entrance and straining to hear every word.

Great.

We all ordered beer and burgers, the waitress staring at us with open curiosity. While we waited for our food, Kelsey smiled at me brightly. "How ever did you two meet?"

Jackson put a protective arm around me and pulled me close. He'd been sure to sit with me, and I found that small gesture reassuring. Under the table, I gripped his thigh with one hand, staking my claim. Even though she couldn't see it, the contact made me feel better and less likely to leap across the table at her.

"I knew she was the one the first time I laid eyes on her," Jackson said. "She took a little convincing though." He smiled at me.

I returned his smile, remembering the night he'd shown up on my doorstep with the promise to 'make me howl.' I'd doubted him, but he'd been right. Jackson had brought my wolf.

"I heard you were a null, Chloe." Kelsey unwrapped her silverware and smoothed her napkin into her lap.

I shrugged. "Not anymore."

"They say nulls are weak and infertile." Her lips smiled, but her eyes shone with malice.

"Kelsey," Jackson said, a note of warning in his voice.

At the same time, I said, "Try me." I'd face her down same as Vicki. As for having babies, who knew, but I wasn't overly concerned about it because, no matter what everyone thought they knew, I had never been a true null.

She put a hand to her chest, an innocent expression on her face. "Oh? Have I said something wrong? Sorry."

I looked at Jackson and was surprised to see he accepted her blatantly false apology. This bitch knew exactly where all the buttons were and had no problem pressing them. Surely he could see that? But from the warm expression on his face, I could tell he was blind.

"What was it you said to Chloe outside?" Jackson asked, aware enough to at least know he should change the subject. Unfortunately, the topic he chose added fuel to the fire instead of establishing neutral territory. "The look on her face was—"

Kelsey cut him off with a giggle. "Priceless, I know. All I said was, 'Are you the bitch who thinks she can have my mate?'"

At Jackson's shocked expression, she paused. "Too much?"

He nodded. "Yeah, that's a little aggressive."

She grimaced. "Sorry. You know me, all action and no

thought."

I sipped my beer, my glance ping-ponging back and forth between them. Did Jackson really buy her brainless ditz defense? How could he miss that her apology was directed at him and not me. She wouldn't even look at me. How could he not smell the desire that permeated her scent? It was faint, but I hadn't missed it.

Wanting to remind her I was alive, I cleared my throat and asked, "How do you guys know each other?"

Kelsey waved a hand. "Jackie and I go way back."

Jackie? I sputtered as my beer went down the wrong pipe.

Jackson pounded me on the back. "We grew up together."

"His momma practically raised me. I didn't know my daddy and my momma, well..." Kelsey trailed off and her facade of good cheer faded a bit.

Jackson reached across the table and took her hand in his. "Her loss, Kels."

My eyebrows went up at the exchange. It sounded like there was some painful history there. A pang of sympathy went through me for Kelsey. I knew what it was to have a shitty childhood without the parents you deserved. Of course, the tiny pang I felt wasn't enough to eradicate my irritation with her behavior so far. Things had never been easy for me, either and I'd managed to avoid becoming a badass bitch. It could be done, if you worked at it. The fact Kelsey had, apparently, chosen not to, spoke volumes about her character. Or lack thereof. At least, in my opinion.

Kelsey nodded and then blew out a big breath. "We got into a lot of scrapes growing up. Remember the frogs in the toilet?"

Jackson laughed and released her hand, much to my relief. "As I recall, that was your idea. I thought momma was going to skin us alive for that." To me he said, "We put a bunch of frogs from the creek in the toilet the same day momma was hosting a Junior League luncheon."

"We stuffed them in and put the lid down," Kelsey added. "Made for a nice surprise just when you wanted to pee. All the ladies of our pack screamed like little girls and ran scared in their Sunday best." She snickered and pretended to clutch her pearls. "You'd think they'd never torn out a rabbit's throat with their bare teeth."

"What about the time we dumped the sugar and replaced it with salt?" Jackson asked with a chuckle. "That was also your brainchild, although momma didn't believe me."

Kelsey made a face. "Ugh. She made us drink that lemonade too. I haven't drank it since. What about you?"

Jackson shrugged. "It's okay in small quantities, but yeah, I can never quite shake the taste of salt and lemon from that day."

She leaned over the table, eyes focused on Jackson as if I didn't exist. "Oh hey, remember when we swore we'd be each other's mates?"

I gasped and stared at her, stunned by her brazenness. *Who* acted like that? Wolves looking for a fight, that's who.

Jackson shifted uncomfortably next to me. "That was a

long time ago. We were just kids."

She tossed her head, flipping her long hair over her shoulder. "Yeah, like I said, ancient history, but for a while we thought we were meant for each other." She sighed. "Those were the days, but now you have Chloe." Her glance fell on me and then quickly slid over to Jackson.

"Yeah, I do." He gave me another squeeze and I leaned into him. "How about you, Kels? You find your mate yet?"

She pouted and shook her head. "Not yet, but I keep looking. You ever hear of Moonpair dot com?"

We both shook our heads.

"It's a wolf dating site. No one in my pack is my mate so I've branched out. That's part of the reason why I'm up here. There was a promising candidate in Nashville."

"Oh?" I asked. "How did it go?"

She looked so crestfallen I almost felt sorry for her. My sympathy didn't last long, though. Kelsey was trouble, I could smell it. If I went soft on her, she would destroy me. Just like Vicki.

Her gaze dropped to her lap where she fiddled with her napkin. "Not a match."

"Sorry to hear that, Kels."

She shook her shoulders and sat straighter in her seat. "All in good time, right? Let's talk about your wedding. Have you made any plans yet?" Now she looked at me, finally.

"I've ordered a few things and looked at lots of

magazines."

Kelsey frowned. "Magazines are so last century. Honey, all the wedding action is on Pinterest these days." Her mouth split in a wide grin. "Don't worry, I'll hook you up. Where's the hall going to be?"

Jackson and I exchanged glances. This was the most we'd talked about the wedding since we'd decided to have one. "There isn't one," I said. "We do outdoor weddings in our pack."

"Perfect. No contracts or fees. Very budget friendly. I approve." She winked at me conspiratorially. "I have some great ideas for the decor."

"I was thinking of a wild flower arbor," I said. It would mean a late summer wedding so we had time to grow extra flowers as well as harvest wild ones at the peak of the growing season, but the pictures would be stunning. I'd been to a pack wedding when I was little and never forgot the beautiful archway of flowers framing the happy couple.

She raised an eyebrow. "That sounds nice, very country, but Jackson's family are city folk. You need a more cosmopolitan twist."

"Like what?"

Her eyes lit up. "Chrome accents."

I made a face, I couldn't help myself. "Chrome?"

"Yes, industrial stuff is very trendy right now. It would be a great contrast with your old-fashioned flowers." Her gaze fell on my left hand as I lifted my glass to take a sip of beer. She reached out and touched my naked ring finger and gave Jackson a speculative look. "He didn't give you a ring?"

Jackson shifted uncomfortably. "It's only been two weeks, Kels. Cut me some slack."

"We're moving as fast as we can," I said, feeling the need to defend him even though I often wondered when a ring would make an appearance myself. I also sometimes wondered if marriage to Jackson was really what I wanted. We hadn't even said 'I love you' yet, which made me nervous. The fact I was nervous made me more nervous. Matings weren't supposed to come with doubts. Not in Huntsville where the divorce rate was zero.

Kelsey locked eyes with Jackson for far too long. "Well, let me know if you want some help." She looked down at her own perfectly manicured hand and sighed. "I'm a bit of an expert on the subject and I know all about diamonds."

"I think Jackson can handle it," I said. The last thing I wanted was a ring that Kelsey helped pick out. I wanted it to be from Jackson alone. "We just haven't had a lot of time to focus on the details.

She leaned back as the waitress set our burgers on the table. "That's why I'm here. Weddings need a schedule and a plan."

"I think we've got it," I said as tactfully as possible."Thanks though." When I blinked I caught sight of my wolf, her hackles ran down her back in a mohawk and there was a murderous gleam in her eye. If Kelsey kept pushing buttons, I would lose it. The last thing I wanted to do was lose control, not when I wasn't sure of my wolf or her strength.

Unlike Vicki earlier that day, Kelsey didn't push me any further and I was grateful it didn't come down to another confrontation. We dove into our burgers and ate in silence. Once I'd finished mine, I excused myself to use the restroom.

As I washed my hands, Tonya, one of the barmaids came in. We'd worked together once, before I quit in anticipation of leaving town. The owner had offered me my old dishwashing job back, but I declined. Alpha's mates had jobs; they worked on behalf of the pack. Soon, I would be way too busy to chase a paycheck.

When our eyes met, she worried her bottom lip for a moment and thrust her hands in her apron's pockets. Finally, she took in a deep breath and said, "Hey, Chloe. How are you?"

I shrugged. "Okay."

"Sounds like you're planning a wedding." She smiled at me and I returned the smile. Tonya was a sweet girl with blond hair and light blue eyes. She always had a kind word for everyone and was the closest I came to a friend during my time as a null.

"Yeah, it does, doesn't it?" My words came out a little less ebullient than I'd intended and Tonya didn't miss the nuance.

"Everything okay? Jackson seems like a great guy."

"Yeah." I ran my hand through my hair. Maybe I wasn't as skinny or fashionable as Kelsey, but I was at least having a great hair day. My sable brown hair still had blonde highlights from the summer sun, along with the bounce and body of a Pantene shampoo commercial. "It's just been a stressful day."

Tonya stepped closer to me and patted my shoulder. "I heard about Vicki. Don't worry about her. Even if she gets Cal to make you prove your blood, you'll be fine."

"You think so?"

She nodded. "You're not an Omega, Chloe. Vicki's just mad that Jackson mated with you and not her."

"I noticed," I said dryly. "I'm surprised she's been the only one to bother me."

Tonya shrugged. "Eh, you know wolves. We're practical. We want to mate with our mate, not worry about a wolf who's already claimed his. People are upset, but we'll get over it."

"*We'll?*" I looked at her, eyebrows raised.

Tonya gave an uncomfortable laugh. "Yeah, well, I...you see, this one night--"

I raised a hand and cut her off. "Nevermind. I don't want to know." I was surrounded, I decided. Simply surrounded by dozens of women who'd lusted after my mate. Now they were even coming in from out of town. If this kept up, I would soon be drowning in angry female wolves. Forget 'Call of the Wild' this was 'Call of the Women Scorned.' I just hoped Jackson and I survived it intact. Maybe a wedding wasn't such a good idea. Maybe we should elope and not rub everyone's noses in our mating.

"Hey," Tonya said, interrupting my thoughts. "I wanted to ask you something."

"Okay, shoot." I watched her, wary.

"Since your momma's gone and all--" She looked at the floor and rocked back and forth on her heels. "I wondered if you'd want to go to Nashville together to shop for wedding dresses? I thought you might like some company."

Her invitation touched me. Tonya was a little older than me, but she'd also lost her mother at a young age in a car accident down in Hudson. Wolves can survive a lot, but not a head on collision with a fully loaded semi. Sometimes I wondered if that was why she was nicer to me than most of the other wolves in Huntsville. Out of everyone, she knew what I'd been through.

"I would love some company, Tonya. Thanks." I rolled my paper towel into a ball and tossed it in the garbage. "I was supposed to go down to Nashville today, but my plans went sideways on me."

"Well, I'm off tomorrow, if you want to go then."

"That would be great. Pick you up around nine?"

"Sounds good."

I left the bathroom feeling oddly buoyant. Yeah, Vicki hated me and Kelsey was a problem with a capitol P, but maybe Tonya's offer meant there was hope. Maybe someday not every female in town would hate my guts with such fierce passion.

Then I saw Kelsey and Jackson, and my bubble burst. She'd moved to sit next to him during my absence. Jackson had an arm draped over her shoulder and she leaned into him shamelessly. I wasn't the only one who'd noticed. Everyone in the bar was watching her, and, now that I'd appeared, their attention transferred to me as if to ask, 'what are you going to do about this?'

I knew this was bad. The wolves watching me, waiting for my next move knew it was bad, but somehow Jackson and Kelsey remained oblivious to their transgression. I stalked across the bar, my gaze drilling into Jackson, willing him to look at me, to read my mind. Anger burned so hot in me, I couldn't even see straight as I made my way back to our booth. Inside my head, my wolf growled, loud as a lawnmower.

"Jacks," I said, my voice deadly soft.

He looked up at me and his eyes widened as he saw I was unhappy. Kelsey pretended not to notice and deliberately snuggled in closer to him. Once again she didn't look at me, not out of submissiveness, but to show me how insignificant I was. I held my hands behind my back to keep myself from clawing her throat out. Briefly, I wondered if other wolves fought their violent urges as much as I did, or if my itch for violence was a side effect of being a new wolf not fully in control of herself yet.

"Hey babe." He shifted slightly away from Kelsey as if signaling her to leave and go back to her side of our booth.

She didn't move.

Afraid I would snap, I did the only thing I could to avoid a confrontation. "I'm leaving. I'll see you back at the house."

Jackson reached for me, trying to grab my arm.

I twisted away from his grip. "No, I really have to go. Why

don't you two catch up and we'll talk later?" My gaze drilled into Jackson's with an unspoken demand: *Get rid of her before I do it for you.*

"Clo," Jackson started. From the way his eyebrows had shot up, I could tell he was surprised at my reaction. He had no idea I was upset or that his childhood 'friend' was being rude. How could a man with the heightened senses of a werewolf be so dense?

I cut him off. "I have stuff to do." Not waiting to hear what else he said, I spun on my heel and walked out. As I went, her high-pitched laugh followed me. I resisted the urge to plug my ears. Once inside my truck, I rolled down the windows and blasted rock music all the way home to clear my head.

As I drove, I saw Huntsville through her eyes. The pockmarked paved roads, the shabby city square and mud splattered pick-up trucks. We weren't glamorous people. Fancy meant washing the truck and putting on fresh jeans. We were simple because we knew better than to compete with nature. Just a few miles up the mountain we lived on, there was a view that even chrome couldn't outshine.

Kelsey had obviously spent too much time in the city to understand this.

4

The second guessing started when I pulled into Jackson's long winding driveway. After we mated, I'd moved in with him. He owned the bigger house and it would've been a hassle to buy mine back. I'd sold it to Cal back when we all thought I was a null. He would probably let me have it at cost, but I liked the fresh start.

My house had held my old life, the one where my parents were dead and I was alone, living on the edges of a pack that couldn't accept me. Letting go of my house meant leaving the loneliness behind too.

I wanted to move forward, to jump toward the future I'd always dreamed of except...I'd just left Jackson behind. Now I thought maybe that was a mistake. I didn't like Kelsey. It was an instinctive dislike cemented by her behavior at the bar, but I shouldn't have left him alone with her. My wolf stared me down in my mind's eye, her disapproval almost palpable.

You don't leave your mate, she seemed to say.

Well maybe if he acted like my mate, I wouldn't, I snarled at her.

She turned her back on me.

"Damn it." I hit the steering wheel. Pulling out my phone, I navigated to Jackson's number, finger hovering over the call button. What to do? Call him and say what? No words came to me so I put the phone in sleep mode and tossed it into my purse.

I wasn't going back. No way. It would make me look weak and that was the last thing I needed to be in front of Kelsey or the gossip hounds at the bar. Not that running away helped things either, but the damage was done. There was no use in compounding it with more bad behavior. Heaving a sigh, I went into the house, shivering as a cold wind slapped my skin.

The temperature had dropped below freezing and the house was just a hair warmer than a walk-in freezer. The big ranch house usually retained heat better, allowing us to save money on the gas bill, but the sun had hidden behind clouds most of the day, refusing to share its warmth. As late afternoon turned to dusk, the heat fled at a rapid pace.

Feeling the chill, I bumped up the thermostat and shrugged on a cardigan. Then I slumped on the couch and stared at the ceiling. At times like this, I missed my mom. Some motherly advice would've come in handy, but I didn't have a mother anymore and Vicki exemplified the kind of relationship I had with other females in the pack. That's why Tonya's offer had been so precious; it marked a change.

So now what?

When I moved in with Jackson I'd worried it would be awkward. We didn't know each other that well, but it had been almost seamless. He'd let me decorate the half empty ranch as I saw fit. Being a typical bachelor, he'd done nothing but buy a bed and a flimsy card table set for eating. I'd purchased the leather couch I sat on and kept myself busy with the fun of playing house with my mate.

I'd brought in my dining set as well as other furniture and selected a color scheme. We didn't argue once over paint colors, although he'd raised an eyebrow at the peach accent I'd selected to contrast with the deep forest green in the master bath. No, we fit together just fine and things only got better in bed.

No, not just better, make that fantastic.

Our problems came from the pack and stray wolves like Kelsey who introduced doubt and conflict. The stares and the gossip got to me. Maybe I *would* be a shitty alpha wife. As wolves went, I was a newborn and what would a baby like me know about leading a pack even in a supporting role? Nothing. That's what. Add in a layer of extra judgment courtesy of Kelsey and I felt about as big as a bug that probably deserved to be squashed.

Should I even be his mate?

My wolf gave a soft, mournful howl at that thought. She seemed distressed by my feelings. Well, join the club, I didn't like them either.

The spit of gravel announced Jackson's arrival. I peeked out the living room window to see Jackson's black pick-up. Relief washed over me. What would I have done if he'd stayed out with her for hours? Lost my mind, that's what. Enough to go back to the bar and humiliate myself with a very public display of jealousy.

My relief was short lived though, as Jackson stormed into the house with an angry scowl. Throwing his keys on the foyer table, he marched over to me, a dangerous glitter in his eyes. I shrank back into the couch and gave a weak smile.

"Hey, Jacks."

"Chloe," he growled. He settled into the armchair across from me and leaned forward, elbows on knees, fingers threaded together. His expression guarded as if he didn't want me to see his emotions, he asked, "Want to tell me what that was all about?"

I looked away, refusing to meet his gaze. "She was--"

He cut me off. "Stronger than pepper up your nose?"

I nodded. I'd planned to say she'd been snuggling up against him as if she hoped she would stick, but the pepper analogy worked, too.

"But also a member of my home pack."

I flushed at his reproving tone.

He continued, "Who I owe hospitality to. Who is like a sister to me. What does it say when my mate won't even sit with her?"

I shrugged. "I did sit with her."

"You ran away," he said, the words harsh, but the tone soft. "Why?"

I looked at him. Jackson didn't appear to be as mad now.

Or, rather, he held his anger in check to give me a chance to make things right.

"Because," I paused scared of the words that were about to come out of my mouth. "She made me feel like nothing." I said it all in a rush.

He spread his hands out and then brought them together again with a quiet clap. "You're not nothing, Clo. You're my mate. You're the alpha's mate. That's about as close as you can get to being a queen without a crown."

That made me laugh, a sarcastic bark. Me? A queen. Come on! I couldn't even get the mail without being heckled. My subjects were in revolt before I'd even ascended the throne. "You make it sound so simple."

He shrugged. "It is, babe."

I shook my head. "No, it's not. Before Kelsey roared into town, I had a run-in with Vicki."

His expression soured at the mention of her name. "She giving you trouble?"

"She says I'm an Omega wolf." The words hung in the air and our eyes met; his concerned, mine running scared.

Jackson frowned. "That's bullshit."

I put a hand to my head, pressing against the dull headache that started to pound there. "I don't know. Maybe that's why I didn't change for so long." What if I couldn't blame my wolf's delay on my parents? What if I was just a big, fat weakling? My wolf growled in my head, causing me to wince as the sound intensified my headache.

"We wouldn't have mated then. An Omega can't mate."

"Can't or isn't allowed?" I asked softly. "There's a difference."

"I..." He trailed off, unable to say. With a sigh, he leaned back in his chair. "She's just giving you shit, Clo. Don't listen to her. Omegas are something like zero zero zero one percent of the wolf population. It's as rare as a perfect diamond."

My ring finger twitched at the mention of diamonds, but I opted not to bring it up. "I think it's more serious than that. She's going to Cal with this. Going to call me before the pack to prove my blood, whatever that means."

He went absolutely still, the way a wolf froze right before ripping out its prey's throat. "Cal won't listen to her. He won't let you fight to the death just because she's jealous."

My stomach sank. "Is that what proving my blood is?" On the one hand, I welcomed the idea of ripping out that bitch's throat. On the other, what if I was the one who went down?

He nodded. "You fight your way through three wolves to earn your place in the pack. It's an old practice. Most packs don't use it anymore. We're too scarce these days to throw away lives like that."

"Well, if enough of the pack complains, Cal will have to do something. She's got a few wolves backing her now."

His eyes gleamed yellow. "Who?"

"All the girls from what she says. Mostly the ones you've

dated."

He relaxed a bit. "That's just sour grapes. Everyone knows that."

I grimaced. He still didn't understand. "Well, did you sleep with Tony, Alan and John too? What about teen girls who've just shifted for the first time?"

He startled, surprised at the idea. "Hell no."

"They seem to have a problem with me, too. It's gone beyond sour grapes."

Jackson fell silent for a long moment, his expression unhappy. "I'll talk to Cal. We'll make it right."

I frowned at him. "I have a feeling I'm the one who has to handle this or it'll never stop."

"Then I'll have your back." His mouth split into a thousand-watt smile meant to reassure me. "I'd also like to have other parts, if you don't mind." Yellow heat flashed in his eyes, radiating across the room to brush my skin.

I crossed my arms. "Jackson, stop looking at me like that. This is serious."

In response, he stood up and moved to sit on the coffee table in front of the couch. Taking my hands in his, he said, "I'm not going to let Vicki ruin anything for you, for me or the pack. She's small potatoes and, whether you believe it or not, Cal's got her number. She can pout all she wants, but she won't get anywhere. Now let it go."

"But," I started, but he cut me off with a low growl.

"Let. It. Go." His fingers caressed my wrists. "Let's talk about more pleasant things, like you naked in bed." The yellow faded from his eyes, giving way to pools dark as fine chocolate and full of sin.

Normally I would be a puddle of wet heat in response, but not tonight. Someone needed to show some common sense. Irritated, I pulled my hands from his and buttoned up my sweater, deciding I wanted more layers between my skin and that smoldering gaze of Jackson's.

Wolves hunt three things; gossip, food and sex. Just then, Jackson had shifted into sex mode. His eyes tracked every movement I made no matter how minute and lingered on my most intimate places. I fumbled with the buttons, feeling on edge.

"What are you doing?" Jackson reached for me again and our fingers tangled, me fighting to button, him trying to hold me back.

"I'm cold." I glared at him.

"Don't hide from me, babe," he said softly. "I'll keep you warm."

Somehow his hands slipped past all my defenses to cup my breasts. On cue, my nipples hardened, eager for his touch. My wolf practically swooned, but I held out.

"What about Kelsey and Vicki?" I said.

"What about them?" He squeezed my breasts, thumbs toying with their tips. "This is what fills my thoughts, Clo. You and your luscious body. I think about you all the time. Naked and hot beneath me." He shook me slightly. "You are mine."

"But who do *you* belong to?" I twisted out of his grasp and resumed buttoning my sweater. "You've got a lot of women who think you belong to them." Kelsey's self-satisfied smirk filled my mind until I felt the hair on the back of my neck rise.

Jackson sighed in disappointment, but let me go. "Let me guess, since we've already talked about Vicki, you must mean the mate business with Kelsey?"

I nodded.

"She didn't mean it." He ran a hand through his hair. "Look, I admit she didn't put her best foot forward today, but she wasn't serious."

"I don't know. She looked serious to me." I wanted to believe him, but he'd failed to pick up on the same undertones of our conversation with Kelsey as I had. Sure, they were from the same pack, but did he really know her all that well? "You said you grew up together?"

"Yeah. She was a pack baby."

I raised my eyebrows. "What's a pack baby?" I'd only just been allowed into the pack clearing for the first time two weeks ago. I still had a lot to learn. More than I liked.

He shifted uncomfortably and looked away. "You know my pack has too many alphas?" At my nod, he continued, "Sometimes after a run, if a wolf is in heat things get a little...crazy."

It took me a second to catch his meaning and when I finally understood, my eyes went wide and my mouth dropped open.

"Isn't that rape?"

He shook his head. "Human logic doesn't apply to wolves brimming with too many hormones for their own good. My dad was there, he witnessed the whole thing. She got lost in her heat and was a more than willing participant. Dad tried to stop it, but things spun out of control very quickly."

"Does that mean she could be your sister?" I put a hand to my mouth shocked at the idea.

"No, I doubt it. Dad's the pack alpha. He could fight his wolf's instincts." Jackson paused for a moment and then said, "Anyway, because we didn't know who the father was, she became a pack baby. She belonged to everyone and we all took care of her, especially my momma."

"What about her mom?" I asked remembering the odd exchange back at the bar. There was some painful history there.

Jackson's expression darkened. "She was married and her husband didn't like that fact that some other wolf knocked her up. She had as little to do with Kelsey as possible."

"Oh wow." I felt a small amount of sympathy for Kelsey. "We don't do that kind of stuff up here." There was no post change orgy, ever, and, if you were mated, you didn't sleep around. Jackson's pack sounded like a Las Vegas bender compared to Huntsville.

Jackson nodded. "I know. Every pack is different. If you had all the alphas we do, you might."

I tried to picture our pack with a bunch of alphas running

loose, but failed. We'd never had more than one or two alphas at a time. The whole reason Jackson came to Hunstville was because there was no one to come after Cal. Since our pack alpha was pushing seventy, he'd been concerned enough to reach out to other packs in search of a successor.

Jackson put his hands on my shoulders. I let him come close this time. "Listen, I don't want to talk about Kelsey or Vicki anymore. In fact, I don't want to talk at all." He leaned down to kiss me.

"They shook me, Jackson," I murmured as I pulled away from his mouth. "Both of them, like a one-two punch."

"I know. I could see it in your eyes, but you are my mate. You can feel our bond, right?"

I nodded.

"That's the truth of *us*."

I waved my ringless hand at him. "But this is the truth too." I knew we were mated down to my marrow, my every heartbeat sang of our bond, but that didn't mean we couldn't be torn apart. He could walk away or I could even be forced out. It was rare for a mating to be disrupted, but it did happen. With wolves like Kelsey and Vicki at my door, I was afraid of what might happen.

He grabbed my hand and lifted it to his lips. "You want a ring?" He kissed my knuckles in turn, his lips soft, his breath hot.

I shivered. "I want *everything*, Jacks."

He folded his hand around mine and pressed it against his chest. "Then I'll give you everything."

5

My clothes melted off my body as I finally succumbed to Jackson's sweet seduction. I'd been fooling myself if I thought I could resist him. We were mated which meant our bodies sought each other out like magnets.

We passed through the house in a blur of urgent kissing. By the time we reached the bedroom, I couldn't concentrate on anything but the pure need throbbing between my legs. A haze of hot lust consumed all my worries and concerns.

The mattress jiggled as he tossed me onto the bed, and he paused to take off his clothes before joining me. I watched him disrobe, my gaze tracing the hard lines of his muscles. His skin was still tinted caramel from the summer sun. The color tempted me to lick him and see if he was as sweet as he looked.

Covering me with his body, which ran warm as an electric blanket, he nuzzled the nape of my neck. I did the same and we inhaled each others' scents for several long minutes. Jackson smelled like fresh earth and pine with a faint undertone of clean soap. He told me once that I smelled like honeysuckle and mud.

I'd been offended when he'd first told me that. Mud? What girl wants to be told she stinks like mud? But then I realized I really liked the scent of wet dirt. True, it wasn't Chanel No. 5, but, with my enhanced wolf senses, it smelled of earth, water and growing things. Mud held potential and the promise of growth. I liked that.

Once we taken in our fill of each other's musk, Jackson moved to kiss me. His tongue traced mine with long strokes. I moaned and thrust my body up into his. My desire was fierce, burning me from the inside out. Fisting my hands in his thick hair, I tried to take over the kiss, but he was not having it and deftly pinned my arms overhead.

"Tonight is on me." He flashed a wicked smile that promised dark delights.

My breath came short and I tingled with delicious anticipation. I was about to be taken by my alpha and my wolf whole-heartedly approved. She actually howled with glee inside my head. When Jackson's wolf sauntered into my mind's eye and head-butted her shoulder, she visibly quivered. His wolf smirked knowingly.

On the human side of things, Jackson kissed me and nudged my thighs apart with one knee. His hard shaft skimmed my belly as he moved down my body. I spread my legs with an eager smile, but he didn't take me then. Instead, he kept moving down until his head was even with my core.

Jackson's tongue breached my core with soft, quick flicks

that teased and satisfied nothing. I gasped, my hips arching up in a futile effort to increase the pressure. Jackson chuckled deep in his throat and pushed my hips firmly down into the mattress. With me restrained, he could have his way with me and I couldn't stop him.

I wouldn't want to anyway. How could I protest when I knew the mind-blowing pleasure he was about to bestow upon me? That didn't keep me from whimpering though, when he drew things out, raising hot pleasure inside me and then leaving me to hang without any release.

When I gave an impatient sigh, Jackson said, "I'm going to take my time, babe. You can fight me all you want, but I'm going to take what I want, when I want it." He then dipped his tongue back into my sweet spot, finally giving me the pressure I craved. He tormented me with it, giving me just enough to almost reach the peak and then backing off before I could climax.

Need clawed through my senses, sparking sensation in every nerve and running in desperate loops throughout my nervous system, trying to find an escape. My hips writhed against the firm prison of his hands, frantic to find an escape.

"Jackson," I keened.

"Chloe," he said, his mouth still against my flesh so that his voice rumbled through my epicenter like an earthquake. Just my name on his lips put me a little closer to the edge.

My hands clutched the sheets, twisting them into handles that would keep me from flying apart. "Do that again," I begged.

"What?" He lifted his head and arched an eyebrow at me.

"You mean this?" He ducked back down and his tongue found my center again. "My mate," he growled, stretching the words out until they were impossibly long.

"Yes, that," I managed to say before my voice disappeared into a scream as I exploded.

It didn't stop there. In the last two weeks, Jackson had learned my body and he knew he could push me back up the peak once more. His tongue stroked me, first in a soothing caress that allowed me to ride the orgasm without interference, but, as it faded, he changed tactics. Instead of soothing, he demanded.

"Are you mine?" he asked. His commanding touch left my body taut under the strain of it all.

"Yes," I hissed. Every muscle in my body quivered.

"Forever," he said as he nipped at me with his teeth, giving the vibration of his voice an edge. The contact was gentle, yet rough at the same time and it electrified me.

"Yours," I said. Goose bumps pinched my skin and my nipples stiffened.

He wrapped his lips around my nub and sucked. I blew apart once again, a wave of pleasure obliterating the tension.

Before I was done coming, he entered me with one smooth thrust. Leaning down, he took my nipple into his mouth and lashed it with his tongue. I bucked at the new sensations piling onto the aftershocks of my orgasm.

It was too much.

It wasn't enough.

"This is all that matters, right Clo?" He slammed into me for emphasis.

All I could do was nod.

"Vicki will never have this. And Kelsey never thought of me this way. You're my mate, no one else. Understood?" Another slam hit me as he sank deep into my core.

I nodded again and he leaned down to kiss me, his warm chest pressing into my breasts, the hair their teasing my nipples. Then he went to my neck and after planting a soft kiss, he bit me. Hard.

It hurt, but I didn't care. The pain just heightened the pleasure of being claimed.

He pulled back after a moment leaving my neck stinging. "There, you're marked as my mate."

I wrapped my legs around him. "Jackson?"

"Yeah?"

"Stop talking and fuck me already." It was time to come again.

"You sound impatient. Am I getting to you?" He grinned, liking the idea.

He was under my skin, in my head and buried inside me, *of course* he got to me. I just squeezed him with my legs, pulling him deeper yet. When I started contracting my core around him, he lost the ability to make smart ass remarks. His dark eyes glazed and his breathing came fast. Sweat slicked our skins as we both chased release.

Jackson had the endurance of an athlete, but no one can last forever. His climax burst in a hot wave and triggered my own. We shuddered into each other, lost and found at the same time.

When we recovered, I snuggled up against his side and he laid a possessive arm over me.

"Jacks?"

"Yes, baby?" His voice was full of drowsy satisfaction.

"What if I am an Omega wolf?" I bit my lip knowing he would hate the question as much as I did. It was just that I'd always assumed my parents' deaths had set me back, but what if that wasn't it. What if I'd been delayed because I was weak?

He sighed. "We're talking about this again?"

"I just...what if I am?"

"You can't be. We wouldn't be mated." He gave me a squeeze. "It doesn't matter, Clo. It's not true and I'm not letting you go."

I wanted to say more, but he stopped me. "Look, you either believe in us or you don't. Are we mated?"

"Yes," I said.

"Then that's all you need to know." He rolled over then and fell asleep.

Still awake, I stared up at the ceiling alone with my worries, which came roaring back without the distraction of sex. I knew we were mated, Jackson knew we were mated, but why didn't anyone else believe it?

6

Morning came with the sound of loud knocking at our door. Jackson and I both jerked upright at the noise. For a second, I was disoriented. My sleep had been dreamless, my body humming with deep satisfaction. Being thrust into abrupt consciousness hurt.

"Jackson," yelled the familiar voice of Cal. He sounded upset.

"Coming," Jackson shouted back. He didn't bother to get dressed; wolves didn't care about nudity and the urgency in Cal's voice said this was not a social visit.

Bed sheet clutched around my body, I trailed after Jackson to the front door. I hadn't been a wolf long enough to lose my human sense of modesty. Being naked in the pack clearing didn't bother me, but, in a more human environment like my home, I struggled with shyness. Sometimes I worried I'd been human too long.

"What's up, man?" Jackson covered a yawn and wiped sleep out of his eyes.

Cal didn't bother to step inside the house. Outside, I could hear his car still running. His usual scent of tobacco and warm green grass filled the air. He always smelled like he'd just cut the lawn while puffing an expensive cigar, but just then there was also a dark undertone of worry to his scent. "Tonya's missing."

"She go out on a run last night?" Jackson asked. Sometimes wolves lost track of time and dawdled until people panicked. The thing was, people worried about schedules while wolves followed whatever enticing scent crossed their path.

Cal shook his head. "No. She was with James until midnight. He said she was asleep when he left. The bar called me when she didn't show for the breakfast shift."

I frowned at that. "She was working? We were supposed to go to Nashville together at nine."

Cal just shrugged. "I don't know. Maybe she picked up an extra shift or was planning to cut out early."

"What about her cell phone?" Jackson asked.

The alpha's mouth thinned out into a grim line. "No answer. So I went out to her place and it's all tore up. Front door's been kicked in and she's gone."

Jackson stiffened and his eyes narrowed. He was wide awake now. So was I and the hair on the back of my neck stood on end. Huntsville didn't have crime. Everyone here was pack and you didn't turn on pack unless you wanted to die. Either something had gone really badly between wolves, or a stranger was on our land.

"Let me put on some clothes and I'll meet you there," Jackson said.

"You do that. I'm going to round up some of the boys, see if they can sniff out a trail." Cal turned and headed back to his truck.

Jackson wasted no time getting dressed and I followed suit. For a second day in a row, it looked like my plans to shop for a wedding dress would fall through. I tried not to read any bad omens into the pattern, but couldn't quite shake a sense of foreboding either.

Tonya had made an overture last night. What if someone wanted to punish her for that? My thoughts went right to Vicki, but I dismissed the idea. Vicki was nasty, but I failed to see how hurting Tonya would further her agenda. She wanted *me* gone, not Tonya.

Shrugging off my suspicions, I followed Jackson out the door. He stopped short, aware of me following him. "Not a good idea, Clo," he said, putting a hand up to stop me.

"What?" Cal's wife, Betty, died when I was nine, but I remembered how she often stood at her husband's side. On the rare occasions he was out of town, she led the pack in his place. Because of my rank as alpha's mate, I had a responsibility to the pack. I wasn't about to stay home. That's not what an alpha's mate did.

Jackson didn't have that memory, though. Perhaps in his pack things were different, I didn't know.

"Stay here," he said.

"And do what? Twiddle my thumbs." I tapped my nose. "I can help track her."

He frowned. "I want you safe, which means you stay home."

I huffed at him and crossed my arms. "You can leave me behind, but I'm not a dog. I don't sit and stay." I shrugged. "Either take me with you or I'll go on my own."

He gripped my shoulders and shook me. "I'll take your truck keys."

I lifted my chin and stared into his eyes. How dare he think he could tell me what to do? "I'll shifter and pitter-patter over there on four feet. Seriously, Jackson, I'm not a child. Don't treat me like one."

"I'm your alpha." His voice carried a growl now. He was mad. Good, so was I.

I gave a sigh of exasperation. "First of all, Cal is my alpha, not you, not yet. Second, the pack sees us as a unit. You leave me behind often enough and no one else will value me either." I pushed his hands away. "Is that what you want for me? Is that what *your* mother did?"

"No." He sighed and ran his hand through his hair. "I just want to keep you safe, away from whoever kicked in Tonya's door."

The sincerity of the concern in his voice softened my anger toward him. I understood the desire to keep me safe. I felt the same way about him. More gently, I said, "We won't be alone, and if you can't protect me, there's no hope for anyone in this pack."

My logic finally prevailed and he gave a curt nod. "All right. But do what I say."

I snorted. "Come on, Jacks. That's over the top."

"Hey, remember you're a new wolf, babe. Running wild is a fast way to get hurt. Just listen to me, okay? It's for your own safety."

"Okay," I said after a long pause where I tried to find something wrong with his logic and failed. God, it sucked being a baby wolf in an adult body. My wolf needed to grow up like yesterday. She gave me a curt nod of total agreement. Neither one of us liked being curtailed.

He picked up the keys to his truck and tucked his wallet into the back pocket of his jeans. "Come on. I'll buy you coffee down at the gas station. I have a feeling we're going to need all the caffeine we can get."

***

Tonya lived out in the woods in one of the few houses that didn't cluster around the town center. Wolves don't want to be separated from their packs and liked close neighbors, but the occasional lone wolf wanted more distance. I wasn't sure how Tonya felt as she'd inherited the house from her great-aunt. She always seemed social enough to me. Everyone knew her and appeared to like her well enough, which made her disappearance all the more chilling.

As we pulled into her driveway, we saw the damage. Tonya's door had been kicked in, left to hang askew on splintered wood. Jackson parked his truck and we both hopped out. We didn't speak, but the glance we exchanged spoke volumes. Something really violent had happened here and it made us uneasy.

My hackles on high alert, I gingerly made my way to her porch, stepping over pieces of broken wood along the way. The porch was new and made of white pine. Tonya had added some nice wicker rocking chairs and a few plants. The chairs now rested on their sides and the pots were a smashed mess of terracotta and dirt. Running my hand over the warped door frame, I inhaled the frigid morning air, wincing as a pungent, unpleasant scent filled my sinuses.

Covering my nose with a hand, I turned back to look at Jackson. "What is that smell?" I could identify most animals by scent alone, but I'd never smelled anything like this. It stung my lungs with acrid air, bringing tears to my eyes. The foul odor was strong enough that even a human would notice it.

Jackson sniffed and then covered his nose too. "Testosterone. Lots of testosterone."

I raised my eyebrows at him, confused. "What does that mean?"

Cal walked out of the house, worry etched on his broad face as he caught the tail end of our conversation. "Rogue alpha."

That meant something to Jackson because he went still as a corpse next to me. I had no idea what a rogue alpha was though and just looked at him with wide eyes, alarmed at his reaction. Behind my eyelids, my wolf stood ready to bolt. She also knew something I didn't.

"You sure about that?" Jackson said, his voice gruff with concern.

Cal nodded. "Yep. I got a call from the pack leader down by Nashville warning me about it. They lost some of their women last week. They tracked him until they lost his scent and he was heading our way."

"You knew?" I gasped, offended at the idea of Cal not sharing this threat with the pack.

He held up a hand. "Hold your horses, wolf. They called me after I left your place this morning." He kicked at the dirt and frowned. "Too bad they didn't think to call sooner."

We all looked at the house in silence.

"So, is Tonya...dead?" I choked on the last word. The thought horrified me.

Jackson pulled me into a one armed hug. "Only if she fought him too hard."

"Nashville thinks he's got a camp somewhere up here where he's taking all the women."

"What makes them think that?" I asked. Cal and Jackson seemed to have a better understanding of the situation than I did. I felt lost, like I'd forgotten to study for a final exam. Rogue alpha was an entirely new concept to me.

Cal heaved a tired sigh and rubbed his neck. "Some strange

wolf bought a lot of camping supplies. He smelled the same as the trail they tracked."

I furrowed my brow. "How would they know about the camping stuff?"

Cal pulled out his iPhone and tapped the touch screen. "The pack down there runs every hunting and camping franchise in Tennessee. They've got wolves working in all the branches and they caught the guy on tape. Someone remembered the scent." He held up his phone so we could see.

I leaned in and squinted my eyes. "Any idea who he is?" The picture wasn't just small, but also of poor quality, probably retrieved from security cameras. It showed a tall, lean man wearing worn fatigues paired with combat boots. Dark hair hung down to his shoulders and a wiry black beard framed his face. Even in black and white, his eyes were wild and crazed. He looked like an off-the-grid militant. I could easily believe he'd gone off the deep end.

"None yet, but the police chief is looking for a match in the criminal databases." Cal tapped his phone and the screen went dark.

Jackson began to take off his clothes. "Let's track him. That scent is so strong, he can't hide."

"Not so fast, cowboy." Cal held up a hand. "I called in our best trackers. Once they get here, we'll go after him."

Jackson paused, hand on his belt buckle. "He's just getting further away. We need to move fast."

Cal locked eyes with Jackson. "I know that and they're coming just as soon as they secure their wives and children. We're also setting up patrols around the city in case he pops up while we're out tracking him. We don't want to leave any easy targets behind." When Jackson lowered his eyes in submission, Cal said, "Take Chloe home and make sure she's got a gun. By the time you get back, we'll be ready to hunt this rogue down."

I shook my head. "Hey, I want to track with you."

Jackson pulled his t-shirt back on. "You're too new and exactly the kind of wolf this guy wants."

I glared at him. "What kind of wolf is that?"

"An alpha's mate," Cal said quietly. "That's what he's looking for. Rogues want to start their own pack and they need a mate to do it."

A chill went through me. "Why take Tonya then? Or any of the others?"

"Because he thinks they might be a match." Cal whirled a finger by his ear. "Rogue alphas don't play with a full deck."

Jackson nodded his agreement. "It's like 'roid rage only worse."

"But if he catches your scent, Chloe, he'd do anything to have you," Cal added.

I frowned. "I still don't get it."

"Not every wolf can lead a pack, right?" Cal asked. At my nod, he continued, "Well, not every wolf can mate with an alpha. You're special, my dear, but you haven't come into your full power yet. Your wolf is still growing and that makes you vulnerable."

I snorted in disbelief. The still growing thing made sense. It seemed every week I had more strength or speed. But special? *Yeah, right.*

Cal chuckled at my reaction and patted my shoulder. Jackson glared at me though and I just rolled my eyes. There he went again, trying to control me. Lucky for him he was so hot and spectacular in bed. Otherwise I would've never had a thing to do with him. My wolf took issue with that thought and gave a soft growl that reverberated through my mind.

Don't sass me, I thought at her.

She tossed her head and refused to look at me. Typical bitch, except for the part where she lived in my brain.

"Come on," I said walking over to the truck's passenger door. "If you're taking me back home, let's go." I still wasn't convinced this rogue alpha guy would be so interested in me, but if Cal was concerned, so was I.

7

Tension filled the ride back to Jackson's house. It irked me to be left out. As for Jackson, well, I couldn't say for sure what he thought, but the way he drummed his fingers on the steering wheel along with the clench of his jaw painted a portrait of a man on edge.

Our ranch sat closer to Huntsville's center than Tonya's house. Not quite in town, but not too far away from it either. It only took us a few minutes to reach the long drive leading up to his ranch house. Gravel spit under the tires and the shadows of the pine trees lining the driveway swallowed his pick-up truck whole.

"You know how to use a gun?" he asked as he parked the truck.

"My Daddy taught me to shoot when I was nine," I said, the bittersweet memory of that day bringing a fleeting smile to my lips. My parents had been gone for a long time now, but I never stopped missing them.

"How good a shot are you?"

I paused in the process of unbuckling my seatbelt. "Good enough." The truth was I hadn't taken out my gun in years. If not for my Daddy, I might have never picked up one. Now I was grateful for his tutelage while also wishing I'd paid more attention.

Jackson stepped out of the truck and, ever the gentleman, came around to open my door. "You don't sound certain."

I shrugged as I slid out of my seat. The driveway gravel crunched under my feet. "I can hit a target. It's just been a while." I looked up at him and my heart stuttered. The mid-morning sun filtered down through the pine trees and streaked his dark hair with light. His hazel eyes reflected the rich green of the trees around us. He was magnificently handsome and I sometimes still couldn't believe he was mine.

I reached out and touched his cheek. Forgetting my earlier irritation with him down at Tonya's house, I said, "What did I do to deserve you?"

He turned his face into my palm and kissed me. "I think that's my question to ask." There was a forlorn note in his voice that gave me pause.

"Everything okay?" Jackson was more prone to over confidence than a crisis of one.

He wrapped his arms around me and sank his nose into my neck, inhaling my scent. His hands drifted to my backside and squeezed. I cradled him against me, giving in to the strong instinct to comfort him.

"Talk to me, Jacks," I whispered.

He groaned. "I'm an idiot, Clo."

"What?"

He lifted his head, but wouldn't meet my eyes. "You saw me. I was ready to run off."

"So?" I'd felt the same urge.

"I would have left you behind." He cupped my face in his hands. "The most precious thing in my life is you and I didn't even think to protect you." He let me go and abruptly stepped back, running a hand through his hair, a look of anguish on his face. "And Cal had a plan. A good plan. I had," he paused to kick the gravel, "nothing but dumb instinct."

"I had the same instinct, Jacks," I said.

"You're not supposed to lead the pack." He glowered at me, but I knew he was more angry with himself than me.

"Neither are you. Not yet." I crossed my arms and leaned against the truck. "Why do you think Cal includes you on everything? So you can learn how to lead." The alpha had Jackson working at all hours, trying to teach him everything he could. "Don't be so hard on yourself."

In response, he pulled me close, shoving me against the cold metal of his pick-up. I raised my hands to push him back, surprised by his sudden movement, but he captured my hands and pinned them at my sides. The human side of me wanted to fight and resist, but my wolf quivered, utterly charmed at the dominant display. When he claimed my mouth in a crush of soft lips and the scrub of unshaved facial hair, a wet heat pooled between my legs.

That's how crazy strong the attraction was between us. Danger surrounded the pack, but we couldn't keep our hands of each other. If that didn't define 'crazy in love' I didn't know what did.

"Don't you need to go?" I asked in a soft voice.

His teeth nipped my neck, adding a new mark to the one he'd planted the night before. "You always come first, Clo."

"But Cal--" I started. He should go, I knew it, but I didn't want him to. I wanted him to finish what he'd started. My core was already overheating in anticipation.

Jackson put a finger to my lips. "Shush. We have a few minutes."

Then he kissed me until I melted. Before I knew it, he pulled off my clothes right there in the driveway and I helped him. Once I was naked, he undid his pants.

"Should we..." I nodded toward the house. A bed would certainly be more comfortable. It would be warmer too, although I found I didn't mind the cool air when my blood ran so hot with desire.

Jackson shook his head and turned me so I faced the truck. With two rough hands he yanked my hips back. "I need you now, Clo." He entered me then, his length thrusting into me with no preamble. I was wet, but tight which made for pleasure edged in pain.

I gasped as he forced himself into my core and even pushed back in an effort to take more of him faster. When he had buried himself completely inside, I wanted to throw my head back in a howl of triumph. Preferring to be discreet--howls could be heard for miles--I settled for a soft yelp.

His hands ran up my back and around my rib cage to tease the tips of my breasts.

"Jackson," I keened. Pleasure burst inside me, popping like so many bubbles all over my body.

"Yes, baby. Say my name."

"Jackson," I said again, my voice ragged. What I wouldn't do for the things this man did to me.

He rewarded me by squeezing and twisting my nipples. Not too hard, but just enough to make my stomach clench. The pressure of the building orgasm ratcheted up a notch. I could tell it wouldn't be long before I exploded.

My hands scrabbled on the hood of the truck, searching for something to hold onto. Jackson's fingers dug into my hips, trying to steady me. My thighs began to shake and my knees went weak. He was so big it felt like he took up all the space inside me. There was nothing but him; he was the sun and my body a planet in his thrall.

My climax started in my stomach and then surged up to my nipples, tightening them into hard points. From there, it washed down to my core where it took on an electric quality that raced over me like a lightning strike.

I bit back scream after scream, only allowing muffled yowls to escape. Jackson continued to stroke me with his hard length and my body kept bursting with new orgasms. Finally when I was sure I would lose my mind if the pleasure didn't stop soon, he gave a hoarse cry. His cock danced inside me and then he went still, sagging against me.

After a while, a howl I recognized as Cal sounded in the distance. It was the call to hunt. I stood up and reluctantly pushed Jackson away. "You'd better go."

He nodded and threw his head back to launch a howl of his own, one filled with triumph. He'd claimed his mate and he wanted the world to know. There was no mistaking that tone.

I blushed and shook my head, mortified. "Come on, Jackson. You're embarrassing me." Shifting made it impractical to be puritanical about naked skin, but wolves were private about sex. At least in Hunstville. Jackson's howl would broadcast our intimate moment across the little valley that housed our pack. Everyone within city limits would know just exactly what we'd been doing. Knowing how many of the women disapproved of me made it all the worse.

Jackson pulled on his clothes and managed to look repentant. "Sorry, Clo. It just slipped out."

"Everyone knows we're together, but what we do alone should be private."

He gave a slow nod. "I understand, but think about it another way. Now the girls giving you trouble know you belong to me. They mess with you, they mess with me."

"Yeah, well, we'll see if that helps or hinders." I yanked

my t-shirt over my head, deciding not to bother with the bra just then. With Jackson on his way out, I needed to get inside and dig out my gun. Moving with quick efficiency I put on my panties followed by my jeans. Jackson gave me a quick hug then, nuzzling his face deep into my neck.

"Be safe, Clo," he murmured.

"You too." I sank my nose into his neck and sucked in his scent. Jackson always smelled like pine and fresh soap. Now that I'd caught a whiff pure testosterone at Tonya's house, I could pick up that undertone in his musk as well.

Becoming a wolf made scent my second language. I'd been barely literate when I first changed, but had rapidly acquired new smells, filing them away in the back of my mind for future reference. The longer I was a wolf, the better I could pick up subtle background scents.

He pulled back, holding me by the shoulders, his gaze searching my face. "A rogue alpha isn't human or wolf, he's just a monster. Shoot first, okay?"

I nodded as he jumped into his truck and waved as he drove off. Alone, the chill of winter crept over my skin like phantom fingers. I shivered and hugged myself suddenly feeling vulnerable. With a start, I realized I'd come to rely on Jackson's presence to steady me. He helped me make sense of being a wolf.

Without him did I even know who I was?

8

" The silence of being alone made me jumpy. Every sound put me on high alert. Nothing like having a violent kidnapper on the loose. I busied myself with some cleaning and laundry, trying not to worry about Jackson. Dinner was a frozen Lean Cuisine with a side salad. The whole day, I kept an ear out for any howls from Jackson or other pack members.

Once, I spotted one of the wolves patrolling Huntsville's perimeter. From the markings on his fur and the faint whiff of oil and gas mixed with his musk, I recognized him as Robert. He was in his early thirties and he worked as a mechanic at the gas station. I gave him a friendly wave and put out a bowl of water for him, which he slurped up in short order. Then, with a nod to me, he melted back into the trees to continue his patrol.

Darkness came like a bad omen. The growing shadows made me nervous. Wolves can see pretty well in the dark, better than a human, but nowhere near as well as a cat or owl. We could be snuck up on, assuming our more sensitive noses didn't catch the scent first.

The blind spot made me jumpy. Jackson was out there somewhere and so was the rogue wolf. I took small comfort in the fact that the rogue's scent was so strong, there was almost no way he could catch any of us unawares. The scent was like a sledgehammer to the nose, but, even so, I worried. To calm my jangling nerves, I popped some popcorn and put in a movie.

Up in the mountains, the internet connection wasn't reliable enough for a Netflix subscription so we relied on DVDs. While I preferred comedies or romance, Jackson liked action movies, and, since I hadn't unpacked all my stuff yet, I went with Diehard. At least Bruce Willis had some funny lines.

A loud knock on the door sounded after the opening credits. It startled me so badly, I almost choked on the popcorn. Muting the TV, I strained to hear who was there. There'd been no car—I wouldn't have missed the sound of tires crunching on the gravel drive.

"Who's there?" I called out, hand going to my gun. I sniffed the air, but, to my relief, I didn't catch the rogue's scent.

"Mara and Sara," came a thin voice.

"Jackson sent us here," added another voice, this one smaller as if from a young child.

Wary, I opened the front door to see two scrawny little girls on my doorstep. Their thin coats were worn and too small. Underneath, I caught a glimpse of equally worn clothes. The taller of the two looked to be about twelve and the other was maybe eight. They both had long blonde hair that needed combing and wide blue eyes that looked to me like they'd seen more than they should. Even though I didn't know them, my heart went out to the girls based on their appearance alone. Someone wasn't taking care of them very well.

The taller one gave a tentative smile as if unsure of her reception. "I'm Mara and this is Sara." Her little sister lifted a hand in greeting.

I motioned them into the house my eyes scanning the world outside for danger. "Come on in and warm up. I've got popcorn."

At the mention of food, their eyes lit up, and, once inside, they descended on the bowl of popcorn like locusts.

"You said Jackson sent you?"

Mara nodded as she shoved another handful of popcorn into her mouth. Chewing and talking at the same time, she said, "We was out looking for our parents when he come through. He told us it ain't safe to be out and your house be closer than Grammy's."

I frowned. "Looking for your parents?"

Sara looked at me, her expression solemn and popcorn clutched tight in her grubby hand. "They be feral."

I tried to act like wolves abandoned their families every day and kept my shock from showing on my face. I knew it happened. Every pack had at least one wolf who got lost in their animal and left the human world, preferring the way of the wild. Usually they came back home, eventually, but, on occasion, a wolf seemed to forget their humanity altogether. From the girls' condition, I suspected their parents fell into the latter category. "Oh, so you live with your grandmother."

"Yeah, she need help now too so it's good we there," said the older one, her butchered English making me wince.

I filed the tidbit about her grandmother away for future reference and smiled brightly at the girls. "Do you want something to drink? Maybe a sandwich?"

Mouths full of popcorn, they both nodded vigorously.

I made them generous peanut butter and jelly sandwiches with a side of chips and sliced apples. Setting the plates on the table, I poured out big glasses of cold milk. "Girls, come sit. The food is ready."

They ran into the dining room, stuffing food into their mouths before their butts hit their chairs. I let the lack of manners slide as the girls were obviously starving. Their grandmother didn't seem to be taking care of them like she should.

Normally, Cal's wife would've paid her a visit and overseen the girls' welfare. When things with the rogue alpha settled down, I resolved to do the same. For once, I was glad of my new role as alpha's mate. It meant I could do something about the girls' obvious need. I didn't have to look the other way.

"By the way, my name is Chloe," I said as I joined them at the table. "It's nice to meet you Mara and Sara."

"Yes'm," the girls mumbled in unison, eyes riveted on their plates, hands in constant motion as they shoveled in the next bite.

"If you want more after you finish that, let me know. I'd be happy to make you another sandwich."

Mara's eyes lifted up and met mine, shining with happiness. "Really?" she asked as if she wasn't sure she'd heard me correctly.

"Yes really. I want you to grow big and strong which means you need to eat. As much as you want," I said, emphasizing the last sentence. "I've got ice cream, too."

Sara went still, the sandwich in her hand suddenly freezing in its trajectory toward her mouth. Her gaze went to the sliding door behind the dining room table and out to the stone patio beyond. "There be somethin' out there, Miss Chloe."

"What?" I stiffened, all my senses on high alert. Squinting, I stared out the glass door trying to spot what had drawn her attention.

Mara pointed. "There back in the bushes. I seen it too."

I inched the door open and sniffed the wind. When I didn't catch the peppery hot scent of the rogue alpha, I relaxed somewhat, but then a feminine, sour stench hit my nose, one I knew very well.

Wolves smell different at different times depending on who is involved and how they feel. It has to do with emotion and the hormones that come with them. Hate always smelled sour as bad vinegar to me and the last time I'd caught that particular scent it'd been emanating off Vicki.

For a second time that night I called out, "Who's there?" Even though I figured I knew who it was, I thought it best not to show my hand. Besides, if I was wrong, I would look like an idiot and I was in no hurry to add to the list of bumbling mistakes I'd made the last few days.

There was no answer, but I heard the rustle of leaves or bushes and the crack of twigs snapping underfoot. I pulled out my gun, and stepped onto the patio, shutting the door behind me. The full moon provided some illumination, but not enough to penetrate the night's shadows.

In a loud voice I said, "I'm armed and I will shoot to kill if you don't identify yourself."

The only response was more rustling and the sharp snap of wood breaking. A chill went through me. Jackson said I would be safer here, that the rogue would be busy running from them. It had made sense at the time, but now I wasn't so sure he'd been right.

A flash of white caught my eye and I trained my gun on it, eyes narrowed, finger tense on the trigger. "Who are you?"

A figure emerged from the shadows. At first, all I could make out was that it was a person and female. This reassured me, at least initially. Then, as they came closer, I made out the sourpuss features of Vicki. My instincts had run true. The nose always knows.

She frowned at me as if she'd just tasted something unpleasant.

"What are you doing out here?" I didn't put the gun back in my shoulder holster, but I did lower my arm. She was pack, not a rogue alpha, I didn't have anything to fear, but I couldn't quite convince myself to tuck my gun away. Probably because, deep down, I kind of did want to shoot her. It would be therapeutic. *And wrong,* I told myself sternly. My wolf yawned in my mind's eye. Apparently, my human morals bored her.

"I went out for a run," she said flatly.

"You know it's not safe to run around right now." I arched an eyebrow, suspicious of her motives. Wolves ran in the deep Appalachian woods, not on the outskirts of our house. Was she spying on me or looking for Jackson?

She sneered. "Maybe for omegas like you."

"I'm not an omega wolf, Vicki," I said, my voice calmer than I felt. My trigger finger twitched at my side and I couldn't keep myself from debating whether I should punch her first, then shoot or shoot her and kick the corpse. My wolf favored starting with bullets. *It's just wishful thinking, I'm not really going to shoot her,* I thought at her. She growled in response. If I had to translate, I would swear she was calling me a pussy.

"Then prove your blood."

I rolled my eyes. This again? If I did take a swing at her, I vowed to do my best to break her jaw and shut her up for a while. "That's an archaic practice."

"It's within my rights to invoke it."

"It's within my rights--" I stopped short of telling her I was going to kick her ass because a strong peppery smell had just smacked me in the face. Remembering Jackson's admonition to shoot first, I quickly aimed the gun in the direction of the smell and pulled off a shot. The bullet went past Vicki's side and my ears tracked its movement as it whizzed through the underbrush to bury itself in a tree trunk with a thud.

Since I aimed in her general direction, Vicki dropped to the ground with a shriek, thinking I was about to shoot her. I was ashamed at how much satisfaction I took from her fear. She definitely deserved some comeuppance, but I didn't like myself when I enjoyed it this much. I was better than petty games, right? My wolf gave me a look. She knew better. Wolves never missed an opportunity to improve their standing in the pack. This was just business, nothing personal to her. She didn't care if Vicki lived or died so long as I came out ahead.

Vicki scrambled to her feet, eyes flashing yellow with anger. Her wolf was agitated and ready to burst through her skin to attack me.

I held up a hand. "Sorry. I wasn't aiming for you."

"That's awfully convenient," she spat as she walked toward me.

I sniffed. "Can't you smell it?"

She lifted her nose to the air and inhaled deeply. "Smell what?"

Did she have a cold? What was wrong with her? "The rogue alpha's out there." I scanned the perimeter, my eyes narrowed to slits. The peppery scent had faded somewhat and moved to the far side of Jackson's property. We didn't have a fence or neighbors. The only demarcation of the property line was the grass stopped and gave way to forest. I hadn't thought he would give up so easy, but decided to give him some negative reinforcement with one more shot. This time I hit something and not a tree. Something that whined with pain and thrashed in the underbrush. Twigs snapped. Leaves rustled and then an eerie silence fell over the night.

"Get into the house and lock the doors," I yelled at Vicki as I sprinted toward the sound. I didn't check to make sure she did as I asked; there wasn't time. Whoever or whatever I hit started to move again. More twigs snapped, crisp as dry bones. A cloud drifted over the moon, hiding the world from me.

I squeezed off one more bullet, relying on my ears to hone in on the target because my eyes couldn't make out anything but varying shades of dark. The third bullet hit home, too. The woods came alive with the sounds of things moving. I thought I caught the sound of another wolf, a soft yip that seemed to come to the far left of where I'd been shooting, but, if there were more wolves out there, I couldn't smell them over the rogue's testosterone. His acrid musk burned my nose like I'd snorted a fresh jalapeno, effectively blocking all other scents.

My heart beating faster than a rabbit running scared, I turned a quick circle to check my back. Vicki had heeded my order and gone inside the house. The girls stood on either side of her, and all of them pressed their faces up against the glass.

More clouds passed over the moon, making the world even darker. I blinked to adjust my vision. My ears strained to catch the smallest sound, but heard nothing. A gust of wind blew, bringing a light flurry of snow with it, and a complete absence of any scent beyond pine and earth.

The rogue was gone.

Wanting to be sure, I ran into the house to snag a flashlight. I didn't say anything, just nodded curtly at everyone as I breezed past them. Outside, I crisscrossed the backyard using the flashlight to shine out into the trees. Other than a freaked out raccoon, I saw nor smelled no one.

Back inside the house, I put the flashlight away and finally felt safe enough to holster my gun. Then I called the police and informed them the rogue had just been in my backyard.

Dispatch promised to send one of the town's two squad cars out my way to check things out. Hopefully that would be enough of a lead to track him down. Hanging up, I noticed that, while I'd been outside risking life and limb, Vicki had helped herself to one of Jackson's t-shirts. She'd also turned the gas fireplace on high and made herself a cup of tea.

I found myself wondering how she knew where to find everything. She must've sensed it too because she gave me a sly smile.

"I hope you don't mind, I helped myself to a few things." She gestured to her shirt. "I always loved this shirt." She ducked her head and sniffed the cotton fabric. "It smells like him."

I took really long deep breath before I said anything. I wanted to rip her throat out. My wolf snarled in my head, the sound as close as a wolf could get to 'paws off my man, bitch.'

She flinched even though I said nothing, although I knew my scent carried the rancid tones of anger, which was a form of speech in of itself. Just to fuck with her, I smiled brightly and said, "No problem. Keep the shirt. Jackson doesn't need it anymore."

"That's not the only thing he should get rid of," she said looking me up and down.

"Exactly," I said, crossing my arms and leaning against the open counter that ran between the kitchen and dining room. "It's like you read my mind." I gave her a pointed look.

Vicki just stared at me, momentarily stunned by my response. When she did start to say something, Mara and Sara started screaming excitedly and pointing to the backyard effectively drowning her out. I hid a small smile as I turned to see what had riled up the girls. Vicki had sure had a less-than-ideal night. I was certain she hadn't planned on facing down a rogue or me when she started skulking around the house. She'd probably hoped to find Jackson home alone and have her way with him.

"It's the first snow," Mara said with a happy sigh.

Sure enough, the tiny flecks of snow from a few minutes ago had grown into big fat flakes. The girls raced to the sliding door and pressed their faces against the glass.

"Do you think there'll be enough to make a snowman?" asked Sara breathlessly.

"That's the million dollar question," I said with a kind smile. The girls' eagerness reminded me of my own childhood. At school, we used to see who could scrape together the biggest snowball. While Hunstville did get snow, it tended to melt rather than accumulate. Winters in our area ran on the warm side. Outside of a freak blizzard—the last one being ten years ago—there was rarely enough snow to even make a snowball.

I looked at the clock and finally realized how late it was. Ignoring Vicki, who glowered in her chair as she sipped her tea, I focused on Mara and Sara, grateful for the distraction. The less I thought about Vicki, the less I wanted to kill her.

"Hey girls, it looks like you're staying here for the night. Go wash up and I'll show you where you can sleep." Jackson hadn't bothered with too much furniture, but he had bought a bed for the guest room. A small thing, but I was happy to have it even though I knew, on one level, that the bed was probably there for guests like Kelsey from his home pack. Without the bed, the girls would've been crammed together on the couch and they deserved better than that.

While the girls disappeared into the bathroom, my attention returned to Vicki who'd slunk into the kitchen and returned with a small bottle of whiskey. Pouring some into her tea, she stirred and then sipped it, refusing to meet my gaze.

I cleared my throat. "What the hell were you doing out there anyway? You want to disappear like Tonya?"

She snorted. "Honey, I'm too strong to mess with. No big, bad wolf can take me. Tonya was weak just like you."

"If I'm so weak, how was it I saved your ass tonight and not the other way around?" I snatched the bottle of whiskey away from her just as she reached to add more to her tea. Screwing on the lid I set it on the kitchen counter. I'd be damned if I was going to let her waltz into my house and act like she owned it.

She shrugged. "Just dumb luck. I didn't ask for help anyway. I can take care of myself."

I pointed toward the front door. "There's the door then." I took no pride in kicking her out. I had a responsibility to the pack and the last thing I wanted was for Vicki to get hurt, but I also didn't want her in my home. Mostly for her own safety. It was becoming more and more tempting to grab her by the throat and shake her into submission.

She gulped her tea, draining the mug. Setting the cup down, she stood. "I'm going."

"If you smell a strong peppery scent, you should run," I cautioned her even though I doubted she would listen. Her default setting in life was bitch set to high. It had worked for her thus far, but I wondered if the rogue alpha would finally bring her down a peg. If he didn't, I resolved that I would.

Vicki waved a dismissive hand. "I've been smelling that all night and nothing happened. There's nothing out there but fear for a wolf like you, Chloe. Leave the night to those of us who can handle it." She sauntered toward the door with a flip of her long, dark hair.

I watched her go, my hands clenched into fists, fingernails cutting into my palms. If the girls hadn't come into the room, I would've launched myself at her, but my sense of responsibility to them kept me in check. I didn't want them to see a fight, not as young as they were. Soon, though, the time and place would be right and I would bring Vicki to her knees. Things were going to change, just not tonight. My wolf huffed in agreement, although she felt some lingering regret about not shooting the bitch.

I tucked the girls into bed, told them a quick story and promised them pancakes in the morning. I couldn't help it, the sadness in their big eyes made me want to mother them. Besides they needed fattening up, they were way too thin. I made a mental note to dig around in the freezer and see if there was any deer sausage to go with the pancakes. The girls could use the calories and fat.

The house quiet, I poked my head outside and tested the air. The scents remained normal; pine earth and some faint animal musk. Nothing to worry about. It was as if Vicki had taken all the trouble with her.

That last thought gave me pause and I stood, frozen in place for a long moment, my mind churning furiously. When Vicki showed up, so had the rogue. She hadn't seemed concerned about it either, and while she was a bitch, she wasn't a dumb one. She didn't want to die. So why had she been out in the woods despite the danger?

Dots connected in my head. Dots I didn't want to see.

The truth was, she would love to have me out of the picture. She'd probably throw a party if I died, but she couldn't kill me herself. Not if she wanted to be with Jackson. No, she needed a way to get rid of the competition that kept her nose clean. Where or how she found a rogue alpha, I had no idea, but she'd clearly brought him to my house when she knew I was alone.

Well, shit.

Stunned, I sank into the couch and pulled one of the throw pillows over my stomach. But I hadn't been alone. The girls were here and they spotted Vicki before she could follow through with her plan. For all I knew, Mara and Sara's presence scared her off. I sure wouldn't want the blood of innocents on my hands.

I closed my eyes and communed with my wolf whose energy was restless. Reaching out I tried to sense Jackson, but he was a shadowy figure in the horizon of my mind and not looking my way. I sighed. Whoever found a way for werewolves to carry cell phones while in wolf form would be a millionaire. We were cut off from each other until he came home.

That left me only one option.

Pulling out my phone, I dialed the police chief's cell. Huntsville didn't have a lot of crime. We usually got along pretty well or solved problems outside human law. The police primarily kept us out of human affairs and gave us an official voice in human law enforcement.

He answered on the first ring. "Mueller here."

"Chief Mueller, I think the rogue alpha has been sniffing around my house and I think Vicki Hannstein might be involved with the situation." The rest of the story tumbled out of me. He listened intently and I heard the scratch of a pen on paper as he took notes.

When I finished telling my story, he asked "How long ago did she leave your house?"

I looked at the clock. It was almost midnight now. "About thirty minutes ago."

"I'll tell the patrol to check for her. She lives about a mile east from you, so assuming she went home, we'll be able to pick her up for questioning."

"Call me if you find her," I said.

"You'll know the second I do."

I hung up the phone and hugged the pillow tightly to my chest. All I'd ever wanted was to be part of the pack. I'd believed that my biggest problem had been being a null, but the truth was, being a wolf took things to a whole new level of trouble.

My phone rang a minute later and I jumped in surprise. Checking the screen, I saw a number I didn't recognize. Curious, I answered. "Hello?"

"Chloe?" asked a feminine voice that sounded vaguely familiar. "It's me Kelsey. Is this a good time?" Her tone was tentative as if she wasn't sure of her reception.

"As good a time as any," I said.

"Jackson called me and told me about the rogue alpha." Fear laced her voice, making it unsteady. "And the thing is I think I smelled it outside my hotel room. Jackson's not answering his phone and he gave me your number at the bar earlier. I didn't know who else to call."

"The rogue's not there anymore," I said, wondering why on earth Jackson gave Kelsey my number. I wanted nothing to do with her.

"What do you mean?"

"He was just here. I managed to run him off. So whatever you're smelling is an old trail or even something completely different." I fingered my gun as I spoke recalling the shots I'd fired and the whine I'd heard as the bullets, hopefully, hit home.

"Oh, wow. That's good to know." She paused and then said, "Would it be too much to ask if I could come out to your place? I don't like being alone like this among humans."

When I didn't say anything at first, she hastened to add, "I know we got off on the wrong foot. Jackson is like a brother to me and I'm very protective of him. I'm sorry if I was out of line."

I'd been prepared to brush her off, but the sincerity of her words gave me pause. Maybe I should give her another chance. It would make Jackson happy. "Normally I would say yes, Kelsey. But the rogue is still out there somewhere and I don't think it's safe for you to travel. Besides, our guest room is full. I'm babysitting some kids."

"Oh, okay. I understand and you're probably right, it's not safe to travel. Are their parents out looking for the rogue?" She asked.

"No." I sighed. "It's a long story, but the basic gist is their parents went feral and their grandmother doesn't seem up the job of raising them."

"Sounds like they're pack kids then."

"Of a sort," I said. Thinking to build a bridge between us I said, "You know I was orphaned at a young age. My parents died when I was eleven. I've fended for myself ever since."

"Jackson told you about me?" she asked, guessing at the reason for my sudden disclosure.

"He mentioned something in passing," I hedged not wanting her to feel like he'd spilled her life's story behind her back.

She was quiet for a moment. "It's not a good way to grow up, is it? Alone and belonging to no one."

"No it's not," I agreed.

"I was lucky to have Jackson's family. His father was a good alpha. He took care of everyone, even the unwanted pack baby." She gave a bitter laugh. "Did you have anyone looking out for you, Chloe?"

"No," I said unable to keep the sadness out of my voice. Cal had tried but hadn't had the time to devote to raising a child.

"Well, you take care of those kids staying with you."

"That's the plan," I said surprised at the vehemence in her voice.

"And maybe you and I can get together for a do-over. I'd like to be your friend, Chloe. I can't promise not to say or do the wrong thing. I came into the world with a foot in my mouth and I'll probably leave this world with it still in my mouth and someone else's foot up my ass."

I laughed. "I noticed, but no hard feelings."

"Great. You've put my mind at ease. I'll call you and we'll set something up, okay?"

"Sounds good." We hung up and I tried to watch Diehard again, but couldn't focus. Between the rogue, Vicki and now Kelsey, my life contained knots I didn't know how to even begin to unsnarl.

So I coped the only way I could, I hosed the house in air-freshener to eradicate Vicki's scent lingering in the air. It wasn't enough, but it was a start.

9

Jackson came home around three in the morning. The sound of his truck, as unique as a fingerprint to my keen wolf ears, sent a shudder of relief through me. I hadn't been able to sleep, I was too afraid the rogue would come back. I didn't want to miss a call from the police chief either, but my phone remained stubbornly silent, which meant Vicki was still out there somewhere plotting my demise.

He came into the house quietly as if trying not to wake me. I ran to greet him and threw myself into his arms.

"Jacks."

He hugged me tight. "Clo."

We just stood there for a minute, soaking each other up. He smelled of sweat and dirt, the musk of a hard day's work, but I didn't care. It was just good to have his scent filling my nose, to know he was okay.

"Did you find him?" I spoke into his chest, unwilling to leave its safety to look up at his face.

I felt him shake his head. "Nothing. The scent trail is cold."

"I smelled him out in the woods by the backyard." His arms tensed around me and I hastened to reassure him, "I shot at him and I think I might have wounded him because he ran off."

He moved to let me go. "I'll go out and look."

Now it was my turn to tighten my arms around him and refuse to be released. "I already checked. He's long gone. I called the police and the wolves you guys set up to patrol Hunstville are trying to track where he went."

Jackson allowed me to pull him close again, his warm arms circling me with reassuring strength. He lifted his head and inhaled, testing the smells of the house. "I smell lots of other people. You've had company. Some of them smell familiar, but I can't quite place all the scents. There's something blocking me." He sniffed again. "Is that...air freshener?"

I nodded into his chest. "Yes. It's kind of a long story." I hesitated, unable to decide where to start.

I took his hand and tugged him into the dining room. "Sit."

He sat at the table and I poured us each a shot of the whiskey Vicki had pilfered earlier.

"What's wrong, Clo?" He looked at me, weary concern shining in his eyes.

"Something happened and I'm not sure if you're going to like what I tell you." I handed him a glass and sat across from him. "The rogue wasn't alone. Vicki was with him too. I think she might have led him here hoping to get rid of me and clear a path to you."

Jackson paused, the glass on his lips as he processed what I'd just said. When he didn't say anything, I continued, "She hates me, Jacks. Enough to kill, but she doesn't want my blood on her hands. That could mess up her plans for you, you know?"

He swallowed the whiskey and gave a curt nod. "Damn. That's crazy."

"Yep. Tell me about it." I took a sip of mine, welcoming the whiskey's warm burn.

"Are you sure?"

I shrugged. "Why else would she be hanging out with a rogue in our backyard? She's not selling Girl Scout cookies. Believe me, I've tried to come up with an angle where she's not trying to kill me and I can't find it."

After a long silence, Jackson surged to his feet without warning, his face dark with sudden anger. Turning sharply on his heels, he made for the front door.

I hurried after him. "Where are you going?"

"I'm going to hunt her down and shake the truth out of her." Anger fired up his voice and the testosterone in his scent became stronger.

"The police are looking for her. You've been up all night. Let them do this for now." I put my hand on his, stopping him from throwing the front door open. "Come to bed, Jacks. It's been a long night and...I need you." I started shaking then, my ability to hold it together crumpling as some kind of delayed reaction kicked in. My mind flashed to that moment in the backyard when I'd taken a shot at the rogue. Who knew what was out there or what wolf would come sauntering out of the wild next? I couldn't bear to be left again.

He wrapped me in another hug. "Are you okay?"

I sniffed. Tears sprang to my eyes despite my efforts to hold them back. "She went through the house like she owned the place. Even took one of your shirts." I took a deep breath. "How close were you guys?" I'd been under the impression that Jackson only indulged in a series of casual one night stands when he first came to town. Vicki seemed to go a level deeper than that. There was something about her behavior that said there'd been more between them.

He kissed me, a gentle press of his lips that was gone before I could respond. "We dated a bit. My wolf liked her, so I thought that meant we might be mates. We talked about it once or twice. The second I brought your wolf, we were over though."

I frowned. "So you say, but did *she* know that? Did you call her?"

He had the grace to look chagrinned. "No I didn't. I guess I thought she'd figure it out when we showed up at the pack clearing."

I threw up my hands. "Way to let a girl down hard, Jacks. Wow. No wonder she hates me." God. He'd essentially led her on. I couldn't blame Vicki for being pissed.

Jackson's expression hardened. "Maybe I messed up, but

that's no excuse to kill you."

"Yeah, but she might not have snapped if you'd manned up and talked to her. She's lost it, Jacks." I whirled my finger by my ear. "Like seriously psycho and she is out for blood. Don't forget, I'm not the only target here. Tonya's gone. All those other girls down in Nashville too." The collateral damage of Vicki's jealousy took my breath away. Was there anything she wouldn't do for revenge?

He rubbed his forehead and sighed. "I'm sorry, Chloe. I didn't know she was going to do this. No sane wolf would."

I frowned. "How did she find a rogue in the first place?"

Jackson shrugged. "I don't know. They're rare and I have no idea how she got him up here without being killed herself. Rogues are the werewolves of legend, beasts that are half man, half wolf and the only language they speak is violence." He sucked in another lungful of air. "I smell lots of people. Was someone besides Vicki here?"

I nodded. "Mara and Sara. They said you sent them?"

Jackson ran a hand through his dark hair, fatigue creating shadows under his eyes. "Oh yeah, I forgot. We ran into them out in the woods. I told them to come here since our house was close by." He shook his head. "I don't know what their parents were thinking, letting them run wild like that."

"Their parents went feral and the Mara and Sara showed up here looking like they aren't being properly cared for. I don't think anyone's been watching out for them. I fed them and tucked them into the guest bedroom for the night." I gave a wry smile. "I promised pancakes for breakfast by the way."

Jackson glanced at the clock on the wall of the entry way. "That's about four hours from now."

On cue, his stomach rumbled and I laughed. "Let me guess, you're hungry now."

A slow smile spread over his face. "Yes for lots of things." His eyes began to gleam with desire and his hands were suddenly travelling my body.

I twisted away from him. "We're not alone."

"We'll be quiet," he promised as he pulled me back into his orbit and cupped my breasts.

"How about some food first?" I asked. I hadn't eaten dinner and the girls had consumed all the popcorn. Jackson wasn't the only one feeling hunger pangs.

He gave a curt nod. "Food sounds good. I could use the extra energy." The wicked smile that split his lips left no doubt as to how he planned to use all that energy.

For a second time that night, I made peanut butter and jelly sandwiches. We washed them down with whiskey and then stumbled to bed, unsteady from fatigue and the buzz of alcohol.

In bed, Jackson cradled me for a long time, hands stroking my hair, then my shoulder down to the curve of my hip. "I thought about you all day. Were you safe? Were you okay?"

I gave a soft laugh. "Same here. I tried to see your wolf, but you were too far away."

"I've heard some packs are telepathic." He kissed my cheek. "I wish we were. It would make it easier to be apart."

"Yeah, that would be nice." I wiggled my bottom against his rising hardness. "Did you just want to talk all night, Jacks?"

He ground against me. "Hell, no. I want my mate beneath me, screaming my name."

"No screaming. Not tonight," I reminded him.

"Okay, fine. I'll settle for a hoarse whisper then." He nuzzled my neck and I turned toward him so we could kiss.

His lips were tender on mine, but soon he couldn't hold back. He ravished my mouth, beard stubble scraping over my soft skin, teeth worrying my bottom lip. Our tongues tangled and I moaned, arching up toward him.

This man made me lose my mind. I couldn't get close enough to him. My wolf seemed to agree and, in my mind's eye, she pressed herself up against Jackson's wolf.

When he moved his attention to my breasts, he whispered one command to me. "Touch yourself."

My breath caught at the power in his voice and my hand moved before my brain even understood his words.

"We're going to make you come together." He lowered his head after that and took a nipple into his mouth while a hand went to pinch the other. Deep, hot places inside me quivered and pulled tight.

Jackson nipped my nipple with his teeth, the pain making me gasp and immediately want more. Releasing me, he said,

"Now, when I go slow, you go slow. When I go fast, you go fast. Got it?"

I nodded, too breathless to speak. A fire burned in me, one that couldn't be put out with water. This little game had me ready to combust.

He resumed toying with my nipple, alternately taking it deep into his mouth and whipping his tongue across the sensitive tip. I kept pace with him as best I could. My nipples became harder and harder, stiffening into high points that begged for more. I squirmed underneath Jackson as a pulse throbbed inside my core, beating like a second heart beat. Soon it would explode and pleasure would spill out, flooding my senses.

Sensing I was on the brink, Jackson intensified his efforts. Bunching my breasts up in his hands to bring their tips closer, he became merciless. Biting, scraping, whipping each nipple in turn until my entire body brimmed with desire. The whole time, he growled, low and soft in his throat. The sound shook my breasts with exquisitely rough vibration.

I came with almost no warning, my body arched and my mouth open in a silent scream. Jackson watched my face and our eyes met, his intent, mine glazed.

When the last of my orgasm faded, he lifted my hand away and sucked on my fingers, beard stubble tickling my palm. Just like that, the orgasm became a drop in an ocean of desire. My body clenched tight with need. I wanted him inside me. The orgasm hadn't been enough, not even close.

"Jacks," I whispered.

"Clo," he said.

I wrapped my hand around his shaft to make my point.

"You need something?" There was a gleam of mischief in his eye.

"You. I need you." I parted my legs in invitation.

When he finally took me, I couldn't suppress a sharp yip of excitement. Behind my eyelids, my wolf was yowling. To quiet myself, both inside and out, I sank my teeth into his neck. Jackson returned the favor and we marked each other. We both crested at the same time after that.

The second orgasm shook me with the intensity of raw voltage. I filled my mouth with the curve of his shoulder to keep from screaming as my body shuddered around him. Jackson grunted as my teeth broke his skin and bit me again as well.

Bloodied, our bodies slick with sweat, we collapsed on the bed, side-by-side.

"Wow," he said quietly. His hand sought out mine and gave a squeeze.

I squeezed back. "Yeah. That was something wasn't it?" I thought for a second and then said, "Was it like this with the other girls?"

"Clo..." He started, sounding unhappy.

I cut him off. "I'm not being jealous. I genuinely want to know. Remember, you're my first."

"And only." He squeezed my hand again, harder this time.

"So answer the question." I turned my head to look at him. Jackson's dark chocolate eyes were heavy-lidded with fatigue and satisfaction.

"No, it was never like this with anyone but you."

"Because I'm your mate."

He nodded. "You're my everything."

The sincerity of his words made me feel a little mushy inside. Even my wolf managed to look sentimental. Instead of her usual boring, death stare, she actually blinked. Maybe she was surprised. I snuggled up against him, basking in the heat of his body. My own body temperature ran on the high side, but Jackson was pure alpha furnace, perfect for a cold winter's night.

There might be a rogue out there and dozens of angry she-wolves scorned gunning for me, but just then, with Jackson's arms and body wrapped around me, his words still ringing in my ears, life felt perfect.

Was this love? Would we last? Was the mating really a thing for us? I didn't know. I hadn't even had a boyfriend let alone sex before Jackson, but, for a brief moment that night, I believed our mating bond transcended anything the world could throw at us.

10

Morning came painfully early. The giggling of the girls woke me and I groaned when I saw the sun shining outside. Some days, mornings should do the world a favor and hit the snooze button. Only good things could come from longer nights. More sleep, more sex...what's not to love?

I hauled myself out of bed and stumbled into the master bathroom where I threw cold water on my face and rinsed the post-whiskey consumption taste out of my mouth. For his part, Jackson just rolled over and covered his head with a pillow, hiding.

I left him be since he'd been running through the forest for hours the night before and needed the rest more than I did. I went into the kitchen where I tried to remember how the hell to make pancakes.

Mara and Sara swarmed me the second I appeared.

"Are you going to make pancakes for real?" Sara asked, bouncing in circles, her eyes wide with excitement.

I nodded, still not quite capable of speech yet that morning, and the girls cheered. Fumbling with the coffee maker, I started a much needed caffeine infusion. While it brewed, I found the pancake mix and blinked blearily at the directions on the box. Why did the words have to be so tiny? They made my head hurt.

A knock on the door saved me from cooking before my brain came online. I went to answer it and found Chief Mueller on the front porch. His eyes were red with lack of sleep and his evergreen and woodsy scent was stale as old bread. The morning had spared no one it seemed, except for small children.

He took off his sheriff's hat when he saw me and held it in front of him with both hands. The khaki brown of his uniform was creased, as if he'd worn it longer than twenty four hours, which was a distinct possibility. "Morning, Chloe. My shift's over and I thought I'd stop by on the way home. This a good time?"

"Of course, Chief." I motioned for him to come in. "I've got coffee brewing. Would you like some?"

He shook his head. "No thanks, I'm hoping to go to bed soon. I'll take some water though."

I filled a glass with water for him and poured myself a generous cup of coffee. Joining the chief at the table I asked, "How are things going? Did you find Vicki or the rogue alpha?"

"No, sorry to say, we have not. We did find traces of the rogue's scent mixed with hers. There were signs of a struggle in the brush and fresh blood. Looks like Vicki's bitten off more than she can chew."

I winced, picturing her at the mercy of the rogue. She'd

done it to herself, but I couldn't help but feel some sympathy. "Were you able to track them?"

"For a bit. The trail goes cold not even a quarter mile out. Cuts off on the main road."

I frowned. "How does a scent just go dead like that?"

He sighed, his face slack with fatigue and defeat. "Damned if I know." He finished his water. "I've got one of my deputies poking around asking questions. So far, we've established that Vicki was in Nashville around the same time as the women down there disappeared."

I sat back in my seat, unable to comprehend that kind of evil. I shook my head. "I thought she was just a bitch. I would have never believed she was capable of something like this."

The Chief nodded. "It surprised all of us. She's young and beautiful, with her whole life ahead of her." He sighed. "But Vicki really hates you, Chloe. We interviewed some of her friends, and, apparently, all she's been talking about lately is about getting rid of you."

I put a hand to my chest as my heart began to race. "Oh my God." It hurt to be hated that much. I was a good person. Maybe not the best wolf, but I was still new and people needed to give me a chance. I didn't deserve to die. I hadn't chosen Jackson, our mating wasn't preplanned just to spite her. Surely Vicki knew that?

Chief Mueller gave me a sympathetic look. "Listen, the other reason I stopped by was to pass on a message from Cal. He asked me to tell Jackson to meet at his house around three. We're working in shifts now, round the clock."

I nodded. "Okay, I'll let him know."

The chief stood up and I followed suit.

"Thanks for stopping by," I said.

He gave me a wan smile, looking dead on his feet. "No problem. You're the alpha's mate after all. Call me if you need something."

"Same here, Chief." I smiled at him. "It works both ways, right?"

He nodded. "Yes, it does." He looked over to where Mara and Sara were watching cartoons. "Those the Klempoff girls?"

"Yeah," I said, filing away their last name for future reference. I'd been so busy feeding them and then dealing with Vicki and her rogue assassin that we'd never gotten past first names. "They spent the night."

He fell silent for a moment, taking in their frayed clothing and slight frames. "This pack's been missing a woman's touch these last few years. It's good to have you. Betty would approve."

"Thanks," I said softly. "I thought I would take the girls shopping for some new stuff this morning and then maybe pay a visit to their grandmother's house. Things don't seem right."

Chief Mueller patted me on the shoulder. "That's a real good idea, Chloe. I've been worried about those girls."

11

The pancakes I made after Chief Mueller left were an
advertisement for the axiom of 'under promise and over deliver.'
I'd promised light fluffy pancakes, but could only deliver over
cooked pellets, half of which tore when I flipped them. It wasn't
my finest moment in the kitchen.

Mara and Sara didn't complain and gamely doused the
pancakes with extra syrup. I tried to make up for the mess with the
deer sausage. Jackson didn't hunt in human form, but the guys who
did passed on some of their bounty to us. Thankfully, the sausage
only required the ability to operate a microwave and I could
manage that much at least.

Jackson joined us eventually and rumbled 'good morning'
to the girls. I told him my plans to take the girls shopping and then
relayed the Chief's message to him, saying what I could about
Vicki without the girls overhearing anything. Jackson wasn't
happy, but he took the news in stride, saying, "We'll find her. She
can't hide for long, now that we know it's her."

We ate breakfast in companionable silence, watching as the
girls inhaled their food like a supercharged vacuum and then made

a beeline for the television in the living room. I smiled as they scampered off, remembering how much I'd loved cartoons as a kid myself. Jackson finished the last of pancakes, even eating the ones that were black on the bottom. I wimped out and went for the sausage, unwilling to eat my own cooking. Then Jackson cleared the table and started loading the dishwasher.

I gave him a quick kiss on the cheek as I took my plate into the kitchen.

He smiled at me. "What's that for?"

"Doing the dishes."

Jackson shrugged and leaned in close to whisper, "I heard somewhere that this is like porn for women. Tell me, are you wet? Does this make you hot?" He made a show of soaping up the griddle I'd used to make the pancakes. Instead of scrubbing, he caressed the pan with long, even strokes, all the while staring at me meaningfully.

I giggled. "Jackson stop."

He frowned in mock outrage. "What do you mean stop? You know what they say, if you can't take the heat, get out of the kitchen." He abandoned the dishes then and grabbed me, pulling me close for a kiss.

My knees went weak as his lips took possession of mine. The weight of his hands on my hips, the way his thumbs dipped inside the waistband to stroke my skin made my heart flutter. My wolf did a little happy dance, her delicate paws prancing on the ground, ears straight up and tail wagging. She loved it when

Jackson was dominant with me.

He came up for air a second later. "Well, Clo?"

"Well what?" I said, my voice breathless.

"Can you take the heat?"

I held his eyes with mine. "Yeah, I can take the heat." I glanced over my shoulder, checking to make sure the girls were still entranced by their cartoons. Then I slid my hand down and massaged him through his jeans until he was nice and hard.

He hissed. "Clo."

I removed my hand and kissed his cheek again. "Wait until you see what I do when you mop the floor." With that, I sauntered out of the kitchen, leaving him slack-jawed.

"Wait. Mop? What?" he called after me, utterly confused. "That wasn't the plan, Clo."

I just laughed and disappeared into the bedroom intent on getting ready to take the girls shopping. I could still hear Jackson talking to himself in the kitchen, completely flummoxed.

"Do we even own a mop?" he muttered as he banged and clanked dishes around.

I shook my head as I eavesdropped, a big smile on my face.

***

Dressed in jeans and a t-shirt topped with a warm sweatshirt, I went into the living room, sitting on a chair while I put on my most comfortable hiking boots. I considered malls to be the true wilderness of the world. Give me the great outdoors any day. Shopping required more gear than any forest. The girls didn't even notice me, completely hypnotized by some kid's show with a color palette so psychedelic it made me wince.

Boots laced, I clapped my hands together to get their attention. "Come on girls. Time to go."

"Where?" Asked Mara, disappointment shining in her eyes.

"Shopping," I said. "You girls need some new clothes." That made them happy and both girls smiled at me. I retrieved my purse from its hook by the front door and slung it over my shoulder. Then I grabbed Jackson's truck keys from the foyer table. His extended cab pick-up could seat four, whereas my tiny Toyota barely held two. "Turn off the TV and get your coats on."

"Have a good time, ladies" Jackson said as he put the soap in the dishwasher. "I'm going back to bed."

I gave him an arch look. "No mopping?"

He grinned. "I'll mop later. The kitchen and then the bedroom." His voice dipped low on the last word and he gave me a hard, pointed look that made my stomach clench. "You're going to beg me to mop."

I smiled sweetly at him. "Sounds awesome. I can't wait."

Jackson made an expansive gesture with his hands. "Oh, it will be the most amazing, fantastic mopping in the universe."

I raised an eyebrow."Jackson?"

He raised an eyebrow back. "Yes?"

"Do you know where the mop is?"

His hands dropped to his sides."Uh no, I don't."

"In the laundry room, next to the washer," I said helpfully.

"So we *do* have a mop," he said with a note of wonder in his voice.

I tried to hold in my laughter, but he was cracking me up with his mopping-as-foreplay shtick. "Yes, Jackson. They really *do* exist." We both laughed at that. Noticing Mara and Sara looking at us wondering what was so funny, I cleared my throat. "All set, girls?"

Both girls nodded in unison and Mara turned off the television. Then they shrugged on their worn coats for what I hoped was the last time and we headed for the door with a quick wave to Jackson.

Outside, the chilled autumn air hit us all like a sharp slap and our breath made ghosts in the stiff breeze. I shivered inside my coat, even overheated werewolves could get cold if the temperature swing was big enough.

"Mom!" Sara gasped as I shut the front door.

I heard the pounding of feet as they rushed off the porch and into the driveway. Turning around, I spotted two smoke gray wolves in front of Jackson's truck, their gazes focused on the girls.

Sara wrapped her arms around one and squeezed. Mara reached a hand out to the other one and the wolf nuzzled her palm.

I came down off the porch and joined them. "These your parents, girls?"

Sara nodded eagerly. "This be my momma. Her name's Mae. Daddy's name's Rob."

The wolves looked at me, unblinking. "Nice to meet you," I

offered. They gave no indication of hearing or understanding me, but I noticed they were more responsive with their daughters. Their mom kissed them with quick flicks of her pink tongue.

I stepped to the side and gave the girls a few minutes to commune with their parents before asking them to get into the truck so I could have a word with the wolves in private. Once the girls were shut inside, I squatted down until I was eye-level. "Your girls need you. You need to come back. They're hungry and their clothes aren't right." While they couldn't talk, they should be able to understand me, and I wasn't going to let them go without say what needed to be said.

Mae whined, a desolate sound, and managed to look ashamed. Rob just continued to stare at me, his eyes unmoved. His expression was blank, as if he'd forgotten he started out human. Perhaps he didn't remember. Maybe he *was* trapped in his wolf form. Maybe he'd forgotten English, too. I didn't know.

My eyes narrowed and I tried again. "I did part of my growing up without parents and it's a hard road. Don't leave them in the dust."

The wolves showed no reaction to my words. They just blinked and then turned in unison to melt back into the forest they now called home. They gave no indication they'd understood or even cared about what I said, but at least I'd tried. With a sigh, I climbed into the truck and found the girls had already turned on the radio, blasting some awful hip hop music that struck my ears like anvils. It made me sad that their parents walking away from them was so normal, it didn't even register on their emotional radar anymore.

I turned down the volume and started the truck. The drive to Hudson would take about forty minutes and I would've been deaf in five if I'd left the music blasting.

"Can I get a pink shirt?" asked Sara, bouncing excitedly in her seat. "Pink's my favorite color."

"I like purple," said Mara a little more subdued than her younger sister. She was probably more aware of their circumstances.

I looked at them in the rear view mirror and smiled. "I'd like to get you girls a new wardrobe. The works. Coats. Pajamas. Shoes. Everything. Any color you want."

A huge smile blossomed on Sara's face and I noticed for the first time that she was missing her two front teeth. Had the tooth fairy left her anything? Somehow I doubted it. A memory of loneliness hit me. I remembered the days of having no one, and my heart ached for the two sisters. Yes, they had each other, but that wasn't the same as having a parent. Not even close.

Halfway to Hudson, a thought occurred to me and I pulled out my cell phone and found Kelsey's call from the night before. Sure we'd gotten off to a rocky start, but last night's conversation had redeemed her a bit and I wanted to give her a second chance while we were in town. I hit the green call button and waited. She answered on the first ring.

"Chloe?"

I hit the speaker button and kept my eyes on the road. "Hey, Kelsey. You got plans today?"

"Nothing I can't change. You have something in mind?" There was genuine excitement in her voice. She sounded pleased that I'd called.

Now I was happy I called, too. "A little shopping. I have two girls here who need a makeover. You in?"

"Are you kidding? I wouldn't miss it for the world. I am the queen of makeovers."

"Great. You're at the B-and-B off route twenty nine, right?"

"Yep. Room ten."

"I'll be there in about twenty minutes to pick you up." After I hung up, I glanced over my shoulder at the girls pleased to see the eager anticipation gleaming in their eyes. "Are you ready for some fun?"

They both nodded somewhat shyly, but their smiles were wide enough to split their faces in half. I smiled too, feeling like I was making up for my awful pancakes among the other things that hadn't gone quite right in their lives.

***

The day passed by in a whir of retail. We picked up Kelsey on our way to the mall. Dressed in a sleek tan leather coat and her hair in a French twist, she looked very cosmopolitan. She greeted the girls with a knock-knock joke and wrapped them around her little finger in no time. She was good with kids, real good. They absolutely loved her. I made a mental note to brush up on some jokes.

From the girls' awed reaction to Hudson, I had the impression they'd never been outside Huntsville before. Hudson was still a small town by most standards, but, with a population of more than ten thousand, it probably felt like New York City to Mara and Sara. The city's main road held more cars than we had people in Hunstville and there were even stoplights. Huntsville was a 'blink and you've missed' it kind of town. Forget streetlights, we didn't even have stop signs.

The sprawling mall really blew their mind, and they ran from store to store with breathless excitement. Kelsey and I instantly bonded over the mission to get the girls set up with proper clothing. It was the kind of thing we wished someone would've done for us.

The entire tenor of our relationship changed. The hostility she'd brought with her when we'd first met was gone, replaced with an easy going charm. I found myself liking her more and more.

"How did you manage clothes growing up?" I asked as I went through a stack of shirts looking for Mara's size.

Kelsey shrugged and riffled through a rack of holiday dresses. With winter coming, all the stores were in hardcore Christmas mode. "Jackson's momma took me shopping. When I was older, I earned my own money and bought what I wanted."

I took in her snug designer jeans and loose peasant top. She had such an effortless style. The clothes were simple enough, in design, but the fabrics and patterns held rich details you wouldn't find anywhere I shopped. I felt gauche compared to her with my dark blue Levis, plain sweatshirt and tennis shoes. "Who taught you to dress?"

She shook her head, a small smile playing over her red lips. "Vogue. I was into fashion as a teenager. I poured over those magazines like it was homework." She held up a green velvet Christmas dress for my consideration.

I shook my head. "Too green."

She frowned and put it back. "I want them to have something nice to wear at Christmas."

"We don't dress up much in Huntsville," I said, eyeing the dresses doubtfully. Not only were they expensive, they were all sleeveless, which made no sense to me. Granted, we weren't in the high North and our winters were mild, but not sundress mild. I could handle the cold, but I was a mature wolf. For little ones, these fancy dresses were an open invitation to hypothermia.

"I know, but it'll make the girls feel special," she said. "How about you?"

Confused, I looked at her. "Me what?" Was she asking me about a Christmas dress?

"How did you get clothes when your parents died?"

I grinned as I finally understood her train of thought. "Life insurance policy and their credit cards." Somehow the banks never realized that dad and mom had died. So long as I paid the bill, no one noticed. When I'd legally become an adult, I'd applied for my own cards.

She arched an eyebrow. "Well, at least you had money."

"Yeah, but I didn't have anyone like Jackson or his family."

"It's a bitch either way, ain't it?" She laughed, the sound full of bitter humor.

I nodded my agreement as Sara came up to me a bright pink taffeta dress clutched in her hands. "Miss Chloe, can I try this on?"

I checked the price tag and winced, but her beaming expression kept me from saying no. Who paid that kind of money for a fluff of fabric that would only be worn once? At least the damn dress had sleeves. Maybe the price reflected some kind of warped sleeve tax.

Once it was on, I began to see why parents shelled out so much money. She looked darling and she knew it. I wouldn't be able to say no to her. It would be like pulling the wings off a butterfly.

Spinning in a circle she said, "I look like a princess. Can I have it Miss Chloe? Please?"

"How can I say no to a princess?" I bowed and then helped her put her clothes back on. Suddenly, price was no object.

After we finished most of our shopping, I took everyone out for lunch at my favorite Mexican restaurant and treated the girls to huge bowls of ice cream. The shy reserve that enveloped them since they'd appeared on my doorstep disappeared. They laughed openly and talked animatedly with us. It really warmed my heart.

Before we left the restaurant the girls excused themselves to use the restroom, leaving Kelsey and I alone.

She added cream to the coffee the waiter had just delivered. "How are things going with the rogue? I've been wanting ask you all day, but didn't want to say anything in front of the girls."

I blotted my mouth with my napkin. "We think we know who's behind it."

She sat up so straight and so fast it startled me. "Oh my God. That's great. So they'll have the rogue in custody soon?"

I shrugged. "I don't know. Tracking him has been pretty difficult. His scent disappears," I snapped my fingers, "just like that. But, I think it's just a matter of time now that we know the people involved."

She leaned over the table, her eyes locked with mine. "Who do they think it is?"

"I probably shouldn't say anything," I hedged.

She waved a hand, dismissing my concerns. "Oh come on, I won't say anything. I'm all the way out in Hudson anyway and I know nobody in Huntsville except you."

I debated how much I should reveal, delaying my answer as I fussed over my coffee, adding sugar and cream. Finally I settled on, "Someone in our pack. Someone who doesn't want me to be with Jackson." I cleared my throat. "Not everyone is thrilled about our mating."

Kelsey sat back in her chair, her mouth an 'o' of surprise. "Oh my God. That's horrible. I'm so sorry." She flushed. "And then I came into town being a total bitch to you about Jackson, just like everyone else. Oh, geez, Chloe. I'm an ass. A total ass."

"It's okay. Thanks for the apology, though." No one else had bothered with one, which put Kelsey ahead of my pack. I smiled at her. "Besides, I think I judged you too harshly." I grimaced as I remembered all the horribly bitchy things I'd thought about Kelsey before I even really knew her. My wolf, wasn't quite as conciliatory, though. She huffed at me in my mind's eye and growled softly. *Let it go,* I thought at her. *Everyone deserves a second chance.* My wolf shook her head and stood up, turning until her back was to me, unimpressed.

"I don't blame you for thinking I was a total bitch." Kelsey's voice brought my focus away from my wolf and back to her. She slapped her forehead. "I mean, it couldn't have been worse if I'd rubbed your nose into cut glass. I said all the wrong things trying to be funny."

I raised my coffee cup. "Well, here's to second chances."

She clinked her mug against mine. "And new beginnings."

We exchanged smiles, but lost the chance to talk further as the girls returned from the restroom. From the restaurant, we went shoe shopping and Kelsey dragged us into a toy store where she bought them each dolls. I snagged some coloring books and crayons for them too. We called it a day after that and I dropped

Kelsey off at her hotel.

"This was fun. Thanks for your help," I said as I pulled into the bed-and-breakfast's parking lot.

"Thanks for inviting me." She turned back toward the girls. "It was nice to meet you Mara and Sara. You be good mommies to your baby dolls, you hear?"

Sara gave a solemn nod and clutched her doll to her chest. Mara did the same but also said, "Thanks, Miss Kelsey."

"You're welcome, sweetheart." Turning back to me, Kelsey said, "Hey I was thinking...what are you doing tomorrow?"

My ears perked up, curious. "Nothing, why?"

"I thought maybe we could drive down to Nashville and look at wedding dresses. Jackson called me this morning and mentioned your plans fell through. I told him I had some connections at La Rose."

My jaw dropped at the mention of La Rose. It was the most exclusive formal gown boutique in the state. All the pageant girls shopped there, which is how I'd even heard of the place. The news stations always highlighted what Miss Tennessee was wearing to the Miss USA pageant every year.

"I probably can't afford anything there." My bank account still held a nice nest egg from my parents' life insurance, but I'd decided not to spend it on my wedding. Large sums of money were uncommon in Huntsville and Jackson and I might want a different house someday. Instead, I paid for all the wedding stuff out of my own savings. The meager amount I'd managed to squirrel away while working at the bar for almost ten years made me a frugal bride.

Kelsey gave a sly smile. "Jackson gave me his credit card number and said it was on him."

I looked at her with wide eyes, both pleased and shocked. "Are you serious?"

Her expression became solemn, but mirth danced in her blue eyes. "Dead."

I almost couldn't believe this was true. Visions of white bridal gowns began dancing in my head. "Okay, what time?"

"Be here at nine tomorrow morning." She cast a glance back at the girls. "You ladies can take care of yourselves for the day, right?"

Before they could answer, I said, "Oh, I'll ask someone to watch them."

"We can take care of ourselves," protested Mara.

"I know you can, but I would rather be safe than sorry." Especially with a rogue alpha on the loose, but, not wanting to scare the girls, I didn't say that last part.

"Suit yourself, but be here at nine sharp," Kelsey said.

I gave her a little salute. "Yes ma'm."

Kelsey laughed as she stepped out of the car. She waved as we backed out of our parking spot and I rolled down the windows so the girls could shout their goodbyes.

On the way home, Mara and Sara pawed through their bags of clothes, fingering the fabric and animatedly debating which outfit they would wear first. I shared their glee, but for different reasons. The wedding dress I'd always dreamed of was within my reach. Excitement bubbled through me and I realized I was glad Kelsey had come into town. She'd finally shown her true colors and they were those of a new friend.

12

The next morning, I hummed as I got dressed and put on make-up. Today I would *finally* make it to Nashville and shop for a wedding dress.

Jackson snored in bed, dead to the world. He'd been exhausted when he came home, and, not only did we not have sex (a first for us), but I don't think he really processed my thank you for the wedding dress. The night shift had been hard on him. There'd been no sign of the rogue or Vicki, but no one else from our pack had gone missing either, which I took as a positive sign. Although I was bummed that we hadn't been able to follow up our mopping conversation from earlier in the day.

I let him sleep while I prepared a quick breakfast of cereal and fruit for the girls. They'd stayed the night again because I didn't want to send them back to their grandmother just yet. Not until I had time to go up there and check out their living situation. Their Grammy didn't come looking for them either, which told me my instinct to keep the girls close was a good one.

They watched cartoons quietly while I prepped their breakfasts and made coffee. Same as the day before, they'd woken at the crack of dawn. I wasn't quite as sleep deprived as the previous morning, but the early hour still required large amounts of caffeine. My body didn't mind as much as my brain. I could be up and moving, but couldn't form coherent thoughts. At least, not until the second cup of coffee.

"Good morning, ladies," I said brightly as I walked into the living room. I'd just filled my mug with a third helping of strong coffee and caffeine jangled through my nervous system like an electric shock. I could feel my brain becoming more alert by the second.

"Morning," they said in unison not taking their eyes off the television. The cartoon was an old Scooby Doo episode and apparently it was fascinating.

"Breakfast is on the table. Jackson is in bed, but, if you need anything, wake him up, okay?"

They looked at me then, eyes wide with fear at the idea of pulling Jackson out of bed.

"Don't worry, he won't bite." I'd forgotten how intimidating an alpha wolf could be to folks.

"Miss Chloe?" Sara asked. "Can I wear the pink pants with the unicorn t-shirt today?"

"Yes, of course you can. The only things off limits are the fancy dresses Miss Kelsey bought you. Those we're saving for Christmas, okay?"

They nodded as they ambled into the dining room to eat.

I grabbed my purse and ran into the bedroom to give myself one last look over in the full length mirror there. Inspired by Kelsey, I tried to up my fashion game by wearing my nicest jeans and a pretty angora sweater in baby blue. Instead of my worn Nikes, I'd put on a pair of calf length leather boots and I'd pulled my hair back into a sleek ponytail. I probably didn't come close to Kelsey's infallible Vogue sensibilities, but I was a fashion plate by Huntsville standards.

On my way out, I called to the girls, "Be good for Jackson. I'm leaving his truck so you guys can go somewhere if you want. Oh, and, if he's not up by noon, wake him up."

Their eyes went wide again. I hoped a day with the alpha as their babysitter would help them bond a bit. Unless their parents suddenly reverted back to human form, Jackson and I would be a big part of the girls' lives going forward. The sooner they got used to us, the better.

***

Kelsey was there waiting when I pulled into the bed-and-breakfast's parking lot. She wore indigo jeggings with black calf boots and a matching leather trench coat. A burnt orange sweater peeked through the opening of her coat, contrasting nicely with her red hair. Bright red lipstick make her pale skin glow and expert, smoky make-up darkened her green eyes. She looked like she belonged in New York, not the rural back waters of Appalachia. Instantly, I felt frumpy and underdressed.

I parked my little Toyota pick-up and stepped out. "Morning, Kelsey."

She flashed a wide smile my way. "Hey yourself, Chloe. How are the girls?"

"Dying to wear their new clothes and scared to death of Jackson."

She laughed. "I used to be terrified of my pack's alpha as a little girl. He was so growly and big. I sometimes thought he might eat me if I was bad. Jackson takes after him, you know."

"He does?"

"You'll meet him sooner or later and you'll have to tell me if you don't think they are twins borne twenty years apart."

I laughed. "One Jackson is about all I can handle. Two ought to be interesting. I guess I'll find out at the wedding, won't I?" I gestured to my truck. "You ready to go?"

"Yeah, but," she held up her car keys, "you mind if I drive?"

"Sure, I just thought since I know the area it might be easier for me to drive."

She shook her head and headed toward her red Corvette. "I know Nashville pretty well. I did some of my undergrad up here."

I followed her and went around to the driver's side. I liked the idea of riding in such a fancy car. It was the kind of vehicle you drove to buy a wedding dress. My truck was more of the hauling equipment and dirt variety. Not nearly as glamorous as the Corvette. "What was your major?"

"Chemistry." She unlocked the car then and stepped inside.

I opened the door and then recoiled as the strong scent of lavender assaulted my nose. Covering my nose with a hand, I looked at Kelsey.

Catching my reaction, she laughed. "Yeah, sorry about that. I broke a bottle of lavender essential oil in the car. You'll get used to it."

"Okay," I mumbled from behind my hand, not so sure I believed her. The lavender was hitting my senses like a hammer. I could already feel the pulse of a headache beginning to pound.

"We can roll down the windows if that'll help," she offered.

I nodded and shrugged off my jacket before joining her in the car. My puffy winter coat made me look like a five-year-old next to her sleek trench coat. At least I looked halfway decent in the sweater. I set my purse on the floor and topped it off with my coat.

Before I'd even fastened my seat belt, Kelsey had started the car and pressed play on the radio, blasting us both with dance music. With an expert turn of the wheel, she screeched out of the lot and headed for the hills.

"Hey," I yelled over the radio, wincing as lavender air poured down my throat. "Where are you going? Nashville's the other way."

She gave an absent nod and kept driving.

I reached over and turned off the radio. "Kelsey, we're

going the wrong way."

She laughed. "I know that, silly. There's something I want to show you. A location you might like for the wedding."

"You've been out in the woods by yourself? That's not safe, Kels," I said using Jackson's nickname for her.

Kelsey just waved a hand. "Eh, I'm not worried about the big, bad wolf anymore. He's probably some short balding guy with a carpet on his chest who couldn't get a date if his life depended on it. Besides, I can only go to the mall so many times before I go stir crazy." She turned the music back on and shouted, "Now, let's go plan a wedding!"

I laughed, giving in to her ebullient mood, and we sang along to the chorus of the latest pop song together. The fall landscape zipped by as she drove faster and faster. The smell did diminish somewhat as we went, although I ended up keeping my window cracked for fresh air.

After a half hour of whipping around the curves of Appalachia, she pulled into a lookout. The valley below had a mix of trees that had already lost all their leaves and the few lucky ones that held onto the last vestiges of fall as if that would ward off the encroaching cold.

I turned off the radio and said, "I'm so glad we are getting to know each other." It had been fun zooming along with her and belting out songs. Lavender assault notwithstanding.

"Me too. Being your friend was essential." She rooted around in her purse, looking for something.

The odd choice of words gave me pause. "Essential?"

"Yes, I needed your trust." She pulled something out of her purse, hiding it in her hand.

"My trust? Why?" The strange turn in the conversation made me uneasy. Where was the Kelsey of two minutes ago? The one who was planning my wedding with me and singing songs like a karaoke star? I wanted her back. I liked her.

"So I could get close enough to do this." She poked me in the arm with something sharp, moving so quick I didn't see what it was until she was finished. Wolves are fast like that. Normally I would've seen it coming, but she caught me completely off guard.

I blinked. The world went blurry at the edges and the middle rippled like a pond, distorting everything in its wake. Even so, I could see the needle she held in her hand just fine. "Wha--?" I couldn't form the word, my lips were too heavy to move.

"Nighty night," she said cheerfully. Her red lips curved into a smile as dangerous as a poisonous apple. Innocent on the outside, full of treachery beneath.

I lost consciousness before the full impact of her betrayal even hit me.

13

When I woke, the sun still shone high in the sky, so I hadn't been out long. I'd been taken from the car and dumped, face first, onto the frosty ground somewhere that felt higher than the lookout. My sense of direction wasn't as good as Jackson's, he'd had more practice, but I could feel the slight change in elevation. Not a smell exactly, but a sensation and a minute change in air quality.

Movement took an enormous amount of energy, but I managed to flop over onto my back and take in my new surroundings. I was in a campground ringed by evergreens. Three camouflage tents stood in a row. Off to the side, someone had built a crude shelter with unfinished logs. The air smelled crisp and clean, like deep Appalachia forest. Not a whiff of lavender to be found.

"Welcome to your new home," came Kelsey's voice. "Do you like it?" She squatted down next to me, watching with open amusement as I tried to form words and move my limbs. All that came out were howling vowel sounds while my limbs flailed like a seal having a seizure. My body resisted movement as if I'd been frozen in place.

She bent down and put a finger to my lips. Her musky, self-satisfied scent filled my nose, cloying as heavy perfume. "Shh. Don't talk. Listen. Do you want to know my secret?" She laughed. "I'm a chemist, Chloe. A very smart one. The event planning thing was just bullshit I fed you guys. Jackson's not too observant and you wouldn't know any better. I figured it would give me an in and I was right."

I made a face or at least tried to. What did chemistry have to do with any of this?

"In fact, I invented the drug I gave you. It's a mix of silver and anesthetic agents that has many interesting properties." She stood up and began to pace next to me. "However, even more importantly, I found that testosterone injections can create a rogue alpha."

She paused and grimaced. "Well, to be honest, I didn't start out trying to make a rogue. The reality is, there are lots of packs like yours, Chloe. Packs without enough alphas and my hope was to help a beta wolf become alpha. We need more leadership in the shifter community, and short of a breeding program, this was the only way to do it. Except, as you know, the experiment had surprising results."

Kelsey resumed pacing, tapping her chin with a finger. "The big question then became not how to make an alpha, but what to do with a rogue one." Kelsey squatted back down beside me and brushed my hair off my face. "So I brought him up here to solve my little problem."

She leaned in close until we were eye-to-eye. "You."

I grunted, a sound that was meant to come out as 'what the fuck.'

Kelsey ignored my reaction and patted me on the cheek. "You're a nice enough girl, honey, but not the mate for Jackson. I'm his true mate, and, with you out of the picture, everything will be right between us."

My stomach dropped. *Fucking bitch.* I did my best to get up and attack her, but all I could manage was more flailing. While I could move, I couldn't coordinate and I'd lost my strength. Worse, when I closed my eyes, my wolf didn't seem to be in better shape. She was awake, but eerily still as if she couldn't move freely either.

"I drove him out to your house the night I called you, hoping to finish you off then, but that other wolf, Vicki," Kelsey frowned, "interfered with my plans." She brightened then, a small, cruel smile on her lips. "At least it wasn't a total loss, he managed to snag that other bitch on his way back to the car. She's just as much of a problem as you are."

Understanding dawned. No wonder she used such strong air freshener in her car, she was covering the rogue's scent. And, if she'd been driving him around, that explained why his scent disappeared. She probably picked him up at the road and drove him back to camp so no one could track him down.

Well, damn.

Another thought hit me, one that made my blood run cold. Mara and Sara had been in the house that night. Would Kelsey have stopped her rogue from killing them? She'd been so nice to them the day we went shopping, but I'd met the real Kelsey and I could see her not blinking if the girls died. That scared me more than anything else that had happened.

"Ronald will be here soon and I'll give him one last injection. Then, you'll be his to play with." She looked down at me, her eyes gleaming with twisted amusement. "He loves it when the girls fight back and he owes you one. You grazed him with a bullet that night. That's what drove him off."

As if he'd been off-stage waiting for his cue, Ronald crashed into the clearing. I smelled him first, that strong peppery scent making my eyes water. When he came into view, I gasped.

He was neither wolf nor man, but some sick combination of the two. Naked, a fine layer of fur covered his entire body. His face was human except that his nose and lower jaw had elongated into a snout-like shape. Claws tipped his hands and a thin tail grew from his tailbone. When I caught sight of his front, I tried to shriek but only gurgled instead. His penis was misshapen and bigger than a rolling pin.

Kelsey beckoned him over. "Hey big boy. I've got more alpha juice for you." She pulled out a syringe from her purse.

He grunted, not taking his bloodshot gaze off me.

"All in good time, Ronnie. Come take your medicine and then she's all yours. You'll like her, she's an alpha's mate. Just what you need, big boy."

His eyes widened and he came over to sniff me. I froze, holding absolutely still, which wasn't hard given the effects of the medication Kelsey had given me. Up close, his scent seemed to steal oxygen from the air, burning my lungs until it felt like I'd inhaled hot ash.

"Ronald, baby, I'm waiting," Kelsey called, her voice wheedling. He turned and shuffled over to her, but his bloodshot eyes never left me.

I needed to get the hell out of here, I realized. The sooner the better. This crazy bitch was about to leave me behind with her science experiment gone psycho. I tried to get up again and my body merely twitched. Desperate I decided to try shifting, but nothing happened. Silver alone was toxic to most shifters, but whatever drugs she'd mixed it with made it worse.

"Are you trying to shift, Chloe?" Kelsey asked, her tone conversational.

I groaned a paragraph of obscenities at her. How did she know?

She shook her head as she plunged the needle into Ronald's bicep. "You can't shift with silver in your system. I designed the drug that way. I can't have you running off after I've gone to so much trouble to bring you and Ronald together, now can I?" She finished giving Ronald the shot and then tossed the needle into the forest with a shrug.

"You two have fun, okay? I wish I could stay, but I've got an appointment at La Rose. I want to have everything ready for my wedding." She smiled at me in triumph. "I'll be back in a few days to clean up the mess."

She started to leave, but then turned abruptly and came back. "Before I go, let me make sure I have the keys to your truck. I'll need to move it so it looks like you never made it to my hotel." She searched my pockets and pulled out my keys with a smirk. "Jackson will be devastated, you know. He thinks you really are his mate, but don't worry, I'll be there to comfort him."

14

Ronald pawed me after she left. He squeezed my breasts and checked me out like he wanted to be sure I was ripe. I whimpered. I wanted to fight back, to protect myself, but that damned shot Kelsey gave me wouldn't let me move.

Wolves can take a lot of damage and heal faster than humans. Even when I hadn't been able to change, it would only take an hour for a cut to seal shut. But we're not invincible. If Ronnie raped me, he'd gut me with his dick. I wasn't sure if I could recover from that fast enough to survive it.

Of course, that was pretty much Kelsey's plan: Let Ronnie play with me until I died. Damned if it wasn't a good one. I couldn't see a way out. I tuned out Ronnie and his roving claws, focusing on my wolf. Maybe she could reach Jackson's wolf somehow. So far, that had never happened, but I figured standard rules did not apply. This was grandma lifting the car off a kid territory. Miracles could happen. All I had to do was believe and try. My wolf just looked at me with wide, distressed eyes though. She was just as bad off as I was.

I growled in frustration, which made Ronnie sniff at my face. His breath smelled of unbrushed teeth. His tongue flicked out to taste me and I cringed. That just encouraged him to do it more, so I forced myself not to react in an effort to dissuade him. My best option at the moment was to play possum and come up with a plan of action for when I could move again.

An unexpected reprieve came when Ronnie seemed to grow bored with groping me and wandered off with a guttural, "Be back."

I could only assume my inability to respond wasn't very thrilling for him. Kelsey had said he liked it when the girls fought back. That had to mean the medication would wear off, right? She wouldn't just leave me here like an inert vegetable and think her plan to off me would work. She was evil, she was a bitch, but she didn't strike me as incompetent.

With Ronnie gone, the chill in the air permeated my skin and sank into my bones until they felt like icicles. It appeared the medication also stunted my tolerance for cold temperatures. Wolves run hot and I was no different, but paralyzed on the ground, my wolf frozen in a similar fashion in my head, I lacked my usual defenses.

Somewhere behind me I heard a moan. It didn't sound like Ronnie and my thoughts went to Tonya and Vicki, the two women the Rogue took before me. Were they here? Were they alive?

Scuffling footsteps sounded and dry leaves crunched.

"Well, look who's here."

I recognized the voice, before she came into view: Vicki. And she sounded bitchy as ever.

She kneeled down next to me, studying me with narrowed blue eyes. I looked back at her, taking in her appearance. She was naked and smudged with dirt. Her scraggly, uncombed hair held bits of leaves.

"Are you just going to lay there?" She touched my shoulder. "Wow, you're freezing."

I made a groaning sound, trying to talk but still unable to form words. This stupid injection was like a full body Botox treatment.

Vicki leaned back with a look of disgust. "What's wrong with you?"

In response, I flapped my hands and looked at her with wide, pleading eyes.

She considered me for a long moment, uncertainty shining in her eyes. Then, with a shake of her head, she grabbed me by the ankles and dragged me off. "I need you inside the tent."

Vicki lugged me inside an army green tent and shoved me onto an inflatable mattress. Covering me with a blanket, she said, "I don't know what's wrong with you, but you need to get better fast. I can't use you like this."

I could only blink at her. If I'd been able to speak, I would've said, 'no shit.'

"At least you're still a distraction." She stepped outside my field of vision and returned brandishing a crude spear made of wood. "I've been working on this all day. Ronnie's big, but kind of stupid. I'm going to kill him. It'll be easy now that he has fresh meat to keep him busy." She smiled sweetly at me.

I rolled my eyes and tried to wave a hand, but, of course, nothing much happened. Although I did notice I'd managed to move my elbows a tiny bit. Relief flooded me. The injection was starting to wear off. It was just a waiting game now. Once I could move, I was going to deal with Ronnie and then kick Vicki's ass until the Omega wolf shit stopped. After that, I was going to hunt Kelsey down.

Vicki thumped her chest with one fist. "*I'm* the star of this story. I'm the one who's going to kill him. I'm the one who survived what Ronnie is going to do to you, but you won't." She nodded when my eyes widened. "Yes, he raped me and will do the same to you. What do you think he's been doing with the women he kidnapped? Having tea parties?" She gestured to her stomach. "He tore me almost in half, but I healed."

I shuddered at the idea of Ronnie raping me. The rogue was so massive, he would gut me like a fishing knife, I had no doubt about it. "What about Tonya?" My words still didn't come out quite right, but I'd progressed from inarticulate groaning to some semblance of speech. Tonya's name actually sounded pretty clear.

Vicki grimaced. "Tonya? She couldn't heal. She was weak like you. It takes an alpha to deal with an alpha. You don't stand a chance." She pointed to the side. "There's a tent out there where he keeps the dead bodies. She's in the pile."

Pile? I was confused for a moment until I remembered he'd kidnapped women from the Nashville pack. They were all dead? *All of them?* I couldn't grasp what that meant, although I knew I was in grave danger. I strained to move again and was rewarded with the ability to raise my arms and flex my knees. My torsos didn't do much. I was a block of ice, thawing on the edges while the center stayed hard. Still, it was getting better.

"Why are you still here? Why didn't you run?" Maybe she was in cahoots with Ronnie and Kelsey and just trying to play me for a fool. In her place, I would've been long gone.

"It took me this long to heal. I've been mostly unconscious and I couldn't walk until this morning."

"It took you that long?"

She nodded. "My body had to knit itself back together from the inside out. That takes time."

Driven by fear, I focused on my stomach muscles, trying to contract them so I could sit up. I was able to lift my shoulders off the bed, but didn't have the control to do anything more. With a sigh, I flopped back onto the air mattress and for the first time, I realized it smelled. Of blood and sweat mixed with dirt.

Oh God. Am I laying in her blood?

Vicki watched me try to move. "What happened to you? Are you paralyzed with fear or something?"

I shook my head, pleased to find that I could. "No. I've been poisoned. I can't move or shift until it wears off. A woman named Kelsey from Jackson's home pack, brought Ronnie up to

Huntsville to kill me." I flashed a weak smile. "You're not alone in wanting me gone. She wants Jackson for herself."

The raven-haired brunette shook her head. "Once I'm done with Ronnie, she's next. Jackson is mine."

"What's your plan?"

"While he's on top of you, I'm going to come up from behind and," she raised the spear and pantomimed stabbing him.

"On top of me?" My jaw dropped. She would let that happen to me?

Vicki shrugged, unimpressed by my reaction. "Yeah. Listen, honey, it's survival of the fittest right now. Do you really think you're fit to live anyway?" She lunged with the spear, practicing. "Once he's dead, I'm going to Huntsville to deal with this Kelsey bitch." She pressed the spear into my chest. "Then I'll send someone up to find your body. You're done, Chloe. You're out of the pack."

"You're so sure of yourself, aren't you?" I tried to sit up again, but my abs wouldn't contract just yet. They tingled though, so it wouldn't be long. "When I can finally move again, I am coming for you, Vicki. I'm going to show you what Omega really means."

"Which is what exactly?" She huffed. "Too stupid not to get caught in a trap?"

I narrowed my eyes. "No, strong enough to take you down."

The sound of thudding footsteps interrupted us followed by

an angry growl. Vicki looked grim as she hid her spear behind her back. "Ronnie's here."

Just as she finished speaking, a large ham hand flipped back the tent flap and the rogue's enormous head peered into the tent, snout first. He sniffed, testing the air and when he caught our scents, he stepped inside with a growl so low, it was almost outside of human hearing range.

The tent had been big enough when it was just Vicki and I, but with Ronnie inside, there was barely room to breathe, let alone move. Vicki and I exchanged quick glances. For all her earlier bravado she looked like she was scared shitless. I didn't feel much better. Especially when he ignored her and focused on me.

He advanced to where I lay on the bed, eyes shining with interest. Grabbing the blanket covering me, he threw it off. Once again, his hands roamed my body, squeezing, testing, seeking what I didn't know. I did my best to act paralyzed, hoping he would get bored and wander off again.

This time, though, he began ripping off my clothes. The pretty angora sweater I'd put on in anticipation of shopping for my wedding dress, pulled apart with little resistance. He split it down the middle and then yanked it off each arm before pulling it out from under me. The bra went next. I gasped when the elastic rebounded into my skin after he ripped the strap apart.

He split my jeans up the seams and then yanked off the button at the waistband. With a quick pull, the zipper parted and he was able to rip the rest of the denim off me. My underwear, he tore off with just one finger. As it turned out, lace wasn't much stronger than Kleenex.

Now naked, I shivered on the bed and fought back tears. This was real. This was happening. Oh my God. He stood over me, gaze roaming my skin. I wanted to cringe, but forced myself to hold still.

My resolve crumbled when he parted my legs. His cock rose up hard and impossibly long and thick, like a battering ram. I cast a desperate glance at Vicki, but she wouldn't meet my eyes. She did silently hoist the spear and edge ever so slowly behind him. Why she was so careful, I didn't know. Ronnie was so fixated on me, I doubted he would've noticed a tornado.

He advanced on me, his weight threatening to pop the air mattress. Vicki stalked him in the shadows, waiting.

I urged her with my eyes to do it already, but she held back. I realized then that she wouldn't save me, she didn't care if Ronnie raped me or if I lived or died. She'd meant every word she'd said earlier. Well, so had I.

I roared up and head butted Ronnie with everything I had. He jumped up, clutching his head. It didn't take him long to recover while I still heard a high-pitched ringing noise in my ears. Even with my shocked senses, I knew I had to move. I needed to stand up because staying prone would be a death sentence. I rolled off the air mattress just as he pounced. His nails pricked the inflated plastic, discharging a loud whoosh of air.

I rolled again when he followed me. I wanted to get my

knees under me and then pull myself to my feet, but the head butt had left me a stunned, which, combined with the lingering effects of Kelsey's shot, was not a good thing.

Lucky for me, Vicki decided to strike. With a harsh yell, she charged Ronnie. The spear caught him in the shoulder. She didn't do much damage, but did draw blood.

Everyone froze. Ronnie and Vicki stared at the tiny rivulet of blood dripping out of his shoulder while I stared at Vicki. There was a beat and then we were all moving again. Vicki yanked the spear out and tried to nail the rogue alpha again, but he grabbed the spear and broke it in half. Throwing the pieces to the ground, he lunged for her, his hands wrapping around her throat.

She dropped to her knees, making awful choking sounds.

I grabbed what was left of the spear and rose to my feet. Sidling up behind him, I aimed for his heart. Vicki's eyes met mine, they were wide and full of fear, but they were also losing their light as she became starved for oxygen. She would be unconscious soon, leaving me and Ronnie alone. Call me crazy, but I wasn't looking forward to any amount of one-on-one time with the rogue alpha.

I took a deep breath and said a silent prayer. Like the head butt, I put everything into my thrust. Vicki was strong and she'd barely broken skin, I was going to have to do better. I just wasn't sure if I could.

My attempt to off Ronnie went better than Vicki's. The spear slammed into his back, pierced his skin and punched through his ribs. Ronnie reared back with a howl and dropped Vicki. He tried to turn around to face me, but I jumped up putting all my weight into the spear, going air borne as he whirled around, taking me with him. The spear slid forward and into the organs underneath his ribs. I used the force of my landing to thrust the spear point up in the general direction of his heart. Then I let go and scrambled back.

"Let's get out of here," I screamed to Vicki who huddled, paralyzed in the corner. Now was the time to run, while Ronnie was distracted by the splintered wood in his gut. I dashed over to her and grabbed her by the elbow and dragged her out of the tent. Once we were outside, she seemed to come to her senses and quickly shifted into wolf form. She melted into the woods without looking back, which left me to deal with Ronnie on my own as he stormed out of the tent.

It had been a stroke of luck to attack him from behind. I realized this as I watched him try and fail to remove the spear. With it still inside him, he wouldn't be able to heal. The only problem, I hadn't killed him and the damage I had done didn't seem to be slowing him down.

He lunged for me, his claws reaching, wanting to pinch me in his grip. I jumped to the side and evaluated my options.

I wanted to run like Vicki, but a quick check of my wolf showed me that, while she could move now, shifting was still a ways off. The drug was taking longer to leave her system than mine. For once, my human form had the advantage, at least in terms of how fast I cleared medications. The downside? I didn't think I could outrun the rogue alpha while human. I needed the speed of a wolf.

So running was out. I couldn't shift and I couldn't hide. My only option was to fight. Or die trying.

Ronnie growled, punctuating my train of thought with an ominous threat. He squared off in front of me preparing to come at me again. I slowly backed up, unable to think of anything else to do. I didn't have a weapon and he was taller as well as stronger than me.

I really was going to die. I was sure of it.

He sprang forward once more, a snarl twisting his lips.

With a scream, I scrambled backward until I hit the coarse bark of a tree.

I'd moved fast enough that he'd missed me, but he was already coming at me again.

Just as I slipped behind the tree, praying it would offer some protection, two slender forms darted forward. I turned my head, following the flash of motion and was surprised to see they were wolves. Narrowing my eyes to sharpen my vision, I realized they were Mara and Sara's parents.

The two wolves yipped a quick greeting to me and then launched a coordinated attack on Ronnie's legs, aiming for his hamstrings. I wasn't alone anymore. A flash of hope went through me.

I almost felt sorry for the rogue alpha as he spun in circles in a futile effort to stop the wolves. They were so agile and quick, he never even saw who or what was attacking him. Every time someone snuck up on him from behind, he was outmatched. He may have been big, but he wasn't a nimble or strategic fighter. For all I knew, maybe the testosterone had stunted his intellect.

While the wolves kept him busy, I decided on my next step. With the wolves' help I could take Ronnie. Maybe not on strength alone, but on speed and strategy. I would give him a wound no wolf ever came back from. Grabbing a stick thick as my middle finger off the ground, I moved toward him, but he didn't notice. He'd worked himself into a frothing, slobbering fit of anger as the wolves danced around him, sinking their fangs into his flesh every chance they got. Blood dripped from multiple wounds on his legs, splattering to the ground in a red rain.

Ronnie swatted at the wolves with his hands, as if trying to crush them like flies. I stalked the edges of the action, waiting for my opening. Mara and Sara's parents barked at me with excitement. I didn't dare take my eyes of Ronnie to look at them, it took concentration to stay out of the rogue's reach.

As if tiring of all the running, the two wolves latched onto the back of Ronnie's knee on some unseen signal. This time they didn't let go, but clamped down. They were going to tear out the backs of his knees and hamstring him.

Ronnie screamed and when he couldn't dislodged them with his hands he dropped to the ground, rolling in an effort to shake them off. The wolves yelped and backed off to regroup.

This time they attacked him where it would really hurt, the massive dick hanging between his legs.

His howls of pain when their teeth broke the skin made me wince. He tried to wedge his hands into their jaws and force them off, but they held on. When he picked up a rock the size of a grapefruit intent on bashing their heads in, I decided that was as good a time as any to act. No way could I stand by and let Mara and Sara's parents die like that. It would devastate the girls.

With a harsh battle cry, I came in close and stabbed the stick at his face, aiming for his eye. The first thrust caught him on the cheek bone and slid off. I didn't even blink as I went for a second strike. I would have to be faster than Ronnie or I would be dead. This time, I got his eye and shoved it through to the soft brain underneath. It took more strength than I would've expected to breach his skull, but I did it.

His jaw went slack and his remaining eye wide as I drove the stick home. Once it was in deep, I jacked it up and down and side to side, wanting to be sure to scramble any brains inside. Brain dead wolves don't heal. They die human quick. Thank the moon.

Ronnie's body went slack and he almost deflated a bit as he sank to the ground, looking smaller than he'd been. Mara and Sara's parents stepped back with a questioning whine.

"I had to do it," I said to them. "He wasn't a normal wolf. You know that right?"

They nodded, showing human intelligence for the first time since I'd met them.

"Thanks for your help. I'll tell Cal and your girls. They'll be proud of you."

At that, the wolves howled and then they faded into the forest, going where, only they knew.

"I hope you'll come back someday," I called after them. "I'll watch out for the girls until you do."

That earned me another howl, one that sounded much further away than it should've been. Alone and no longer in imminent danger, I began to register my injuries. My arms ached like I'd been bench pressing a semi carrying an overweight load. Somehow I'd twisted my knee and my body was covered in dozens of small cuts and abrasions.

Yet, despite my injuries, a euphoric satisfaction filled me. All along Vicki had said I was weak. I hadn't been sure I was strong enough myself. Not until I killed a rogue alpha with my bare hands. I'd done it. *Me.* The newborn wolf who hadn't even grown into her full power. My fear that Vicki had been right, that I really was an Omega dissipated. For the first time since I'd changed, I felt sure of myself.

I was the alpha's mate, damn it and nothing could stop me now.

I threw back my head and howled loud and proud, not caring who heard me. Hell, I *wanted* to be heard. Let Vicki and Kelsey hear me and tremble to know I was coming for them next. If they were smart, they would start running. They wouldn't get far with me after them, but let them try.

Before I left the camp, I checked for survivors, hoping against hope for a happy ending for everyone. I found Tonya's limp body in the tent Vicky had said held the dead. Sure enough, she'd left this world for the next, her stomach split open like rotten fruit. There were three other bodies too, the women from Nashville. All my earlier euphoria deserted me as I faced the sober reality of their deaths.

I said a little prayer for them all, gulping back sobs as I did so. Tonya had almost been a friend, my only one. The loss hurt.

Fighting for control of my emotions, I made sure Ronnie was truly dead by cutting off his head. I used a hunting knife I found in what I assumed was the tent he slept in and sawed and hacked my way through his flesh. I wasn't squeamish. I'd eaten my share of freshly killed rabbits, their bodies warm and their tiny hearts practically beating against my tongue, but chopping up a human like so much meat made me queasy. I coped by closing my eyes, holding my breath, and taking lots of breaks to walk into the nearby woods to deeply inhale the scent of pine.

Once I was done, I grabbed Ronnie's head by the hair and made my way to the nearest road. Without clothes, hiking through the woods would be difficult. My best bet was to run into someone from Hunstville. Luckily, my thinking was sound and a search party found me a few miles into my walk.

A gray Ford pick-up squealed to a stop next to me. I stopped walking, waiting to see who it was.

Todd, one of the bartenders in town, hopped out of his

truck along with Frank, one of the younger wolves from the pack. "Chloe! You're alive!"

"Yep. I'm alive." I held up the head. "He isn't. Not anymore."

Todd gave a low whistle. "Damn. That's the rogue?"

I nodded.

Frank shook his head. "Shit. You kill him, girl?" Frank ran on the edges of Vicki's social circle and he sounded suspicious. He probably believed all the Omega shit she was spewing.

"Yep." I stared at Frank until he looked away. "Where's Jackson?" I needed to smell him, to feel his arms around me. It had been a long fucking day and I wanted my mate.

"Downtown. Vicki came in about an hour ago," Todd said.

"She seemed to think you was dead," added Frank.

I shrugged. "She thinks a lot of things that aren't true." I shivered as a cold wind brushed over me. "You guys got a blanket?" I wanted to ask them about Kelsey, but that was a sensitive subject. I didn't want to start any talk, not until I spoke to Jackson and Cal first. If Vicki hadn't told them about the bitch, I would.

"Yeah, yeah. Sorry." Todd hustled to the back of his truck and pulled out a thick fleece blanket. "Jackson will kill me if you get sick."

"And what should I do with this?" I lifted the head again, holding the fleece around me with one hand. The guys' eyes went wide as they took in the severed head.

"I've got a box you can use. We'll stow it in the bed." Todd dumped some stuff from a plastic milk crate and held it for me as I set the head inside. He stashed it in the pick-up bed and secured it in place with a few bungee cords. "We don't want it rolling around like a bowling ball."

"Great. Thanks." I looked at Todd's truck. It was an old two-seater. The big console in the middle wouldn't let a third sit comfortably. "So Frank, I guess you're sitting in the back with the head."

He glared at me, sullen, but I just stared him down again. I was the alpha's mate, no matter what lies Vicki spread. I outranked him and since I'd pretty much killed Ronnie single-handedly, Frank couldn't match me on strength. Maybe when I'd first started shifting, I'd been weak, but not anymore. Now I suspected I was stronger than most of the pack except for Jackson and Cal. I'd come into my own, and just in the nick of time, too.

With a long-suffering sigh, Frank jumped into the back of the truck and sat next to the milk crate. Todd and I went to our seats and we headed for Huntsville at top speed.

15

It seemed everyone in town had gathered in front of city hall. Cal and Jackson were there, talking to Vicki who had a blanket wrapped around her shoulders. Some men held Kelsey off to the side. So Vicki had told them or Kelsey revealed herself somehow. Either way.

The entire assembly fell silent at my appearance. The rogue alpha's head in hand, I walked through the throngs of people toward Jackson. I wanted to drop Ronnie's head and run to my mate, my wolf actually demanded that I do so, but I resisted. If we'd been alone, I would've chosen differently, but with so many wolves around, I had to settle pack business first. Hysterical female reactions and tearful reunions would have to wait.

"You okay, Clo?" Jackson reached for me, but I side stepped him.

"I think so." My voice was shaky. "I take it Vicki told you about Kelsey."

"Yeah." He wanted to touch me, I could see it in the tension of his shoulders, but he held back, respecting my need for space.

"And how she turned tail and ran, leaving me behind?"

"I didn't turn tail, you were dead. At least I thought you were," Vicki said, her voice strong with certainty, but her eyes shifted back and forth, uneasy with the lie.

I didn't respond for a second. The crowd waited, holding their collective breath, wondering what would happen next. Very gently, I set Ronnie's head down on the sidewalk and then walked over to where Vicki stood.

I just looked at her, my gaze boring into hers with the full weight of my wolf behind it. She fought me, tried to match me, but, in the end, she lowered her head too. Just like Frank had.

"Tell the truth, Vicki."

"I am." This time she sounded less certain and more desperate.

My hand lashed out, fast as an angry rattler and grabbed her by the throat. I tossed the blanket wrapped around her to the ground and dragged her over to where Jackson and Cal stood. There, I forced her to her knees. Then I let her go...to a point. I pushed my foot into her back, shoving her to the ground. The last thing anyone needed was Vicki loose and running amuck. She'd done enough of that already.

"Let me go, you bitch." She tried to rise, but I held her in place.

"No. Not until you tell the truth." I leaned down and said more quietly, "If you don't start talking, I'm going to take your blood challenge and give Ronnie another head to keep him company."

She went still and I could almost see the wheels spinning in her head as she tried to think of a way out. After several long minutes, she finally capitulated. "Fine."

"Great."

She attempted to stand, but I wouldn't let her. "Can I get up while I talk?"

"No." She'd lost the right to any dignity when she'd left me to face Ronnie alone.

Vicki gave an aggravated sigh. "Fine. Okay. First, I take back the accusation that Chloe is an Omega wolf. Second, when I saw an opening, I ran. I-I-I--" She faltered and I ground my foot into her spine causing her to gasp. "I left Chloe behind," she finally spit out.

The crowd murmured, shocked by her words. To leave pack behind like that was a serious offense. If you didn't look out for the pack, the pack wouldn't look out for you. Granted, I was no expert, but even I knew that much. Vicki may as well be a lone wolf now. Hunstville wouldn't acknowledge her at all.

I stepped back then and let her stand. To Cal, I said, "What do you think?"

Cal moved to stand in front of Vicki, a stricken expression on his face. This hurt him and I almost felt bad for having forced the issue, but, in order for the pack to be strong, wolves like Vicki couldn't be allowed to stand. Cal knew that, but the knowledge didn't make it any easier. Vicki wouldn't even look at him. She just hung her head and stared at the ground. Defeated.

"Vicki you have betrayed your pack. You have spread lies. You turned your back on wolves in need and put all of us in danger with your actions." Cal heaved a sigh. He looked older, as if the last few days had aged him another decade. "And it's my fault."

Everyone gasped, almost in unison.

"I was the one who encouraged Jackson to date the women of our pack. I was the one who wouldn't let him follow his instincts. I was wrong and my mistake has led to a lot of bad feelings." He put a finger under Vicki's chin and forced her to look up and meet his gaze. "Vicki, you have to let go of your anger. Chloe is not your enemy. Stop pining for Jackson, he'll never be your mate, not even if Chloe dies. Go find your mate if you want happiness and stop trying to destroy someone else's. Understood?"

She nodded mutely.

"Normally, we would cast you out of the pack, but I'm going to give you a second chance."

Vicki's eyes went wide.

"I release you to the pack," He said, giving her formal permission to leave.

Vicki took one stumbling step backward, away from the alpha and then stopped, unsure. From the way she kept blinking, I wondered if she was having a hard time believing she was free to go. After a moment, she slunk off, joining up with her usual cronies, who surrounded her like a protective cocoon and escorted her out of the town square.

The crowd watched her go in stunned silence. They'd expected Vicki to be executed, or at the very least, run out of town.

Cal looked out at everyone, his expression serious. "I'm giving all of us a second chance. Many of you have not done right by Chloe. I let it go thinking it would pass, but it's clearly too dangerous to be allowed to fester. She is your Alpha's Mate and you will respect her." He nodded toward the rogue alpha's head which stared out with glazed eyes. "If that doesn't make you toe the line and give her the respect she deserves, then you have earned the consequences of your actions and none of us will have any sympathy for you."

"The same goes for me, just in case there was any doubt," Jackson added, his voice a deep growl.

'Thank you' I mouthed to both men.

Cal smiled, the expression softening his features. "Chloe, I knew you were the Alpha's Mate from the second you showed up at my place after you first shifted. You honor us and I hope we'll prove ourselves worthy to be your pack."

"Thank you, Cal." I went to him and kissed him on the cheek. Then I sank back into Jackson's arms and we kissed. Finally. My wolf gave a happy yip, thrilled to be reunited with her mate.

"I was so scared, Clo," he whispered. "I couldn't see your wolf anymore. I thought you were dead."

"I know. It's okay." I kissed him. "I'm safe, Jacks."

He nuzzled my neck inhaling deeply. "Thank, God."

"There's only one problem."

"What's that?" He lifted his head and frowned at me, concerned.

I pitched my voice as low as I could and pressed my mouth against his ear. "I can't seem to shift. I think my wolf is stuck again. Kelsey did something to me."

"I'll kill her." His body tightened as he prepared to spring toward her.

"No." I laid my hands on his chest and pushed him back. Without question, I wanted Kelsey gone. Dead or alive, it didn't matter much to me, but she'd been like a sister to him when they were kids. I didn't want her blood on his hands. "I'll deal with her."

Reluctantly, I left the warm safety of Jackson's embrace and went to face Kelsey. In my mind's eye, my wolf bared her teeth, her body vibrating with growl after growl. For her part, Kelsey greeted me with a haughty, defiant expression.

Without a word, I hauled back and slapped her across the face. Maybe I couldn't shift, but my werewolf strength had stayed with me. Her head snapped back with the force of my hit, and, when she righted herself, blood dripped from her lip.

"Hello to you too, Chloe." She drew out my name in a sing-song voice, taunting me.

I slapped her again, infuriated by her insolence. "You've lost the right to know me, bitch. Say my name again and see what happens." Grabbing her by the hair, I yanked her down until we were at eye level. "Now, tell me about that drug you gave me. How long does it take to wear off?"

"A couple hours." She smiled, a wicked glint in her eye. "Why? Are you having problems with your wolf?"

I tightened my grip on her hair in warning, giving her a little shake. If Kelsey was smart, she would shut up while the shutting up was good. But, while she winced, she kept talking. Louder now, just to be sure everyone could hear.

"About one percent of patients will find their wolves permanently stunted. Did that happen to you? Aww, poor baby. What kind of alpha's mate can't shift?" She laughed with sick delight.

Her words hit me like a punch to the gut. I'd come full circle, from supposed null to alpha's mate and back. Cold fear shivered through me. Was I going to lose Jackson over this? Would Huntsville stand with me if the damage was permanent?

Suddenly, Cal was next to me with no warning, moving super fast. He clamped a hand around Kelsey's neck. "The kind of alpha's mate who saves her pack."

With a quick twist of his arm, he ripped her throat out. Just like that. One second she was alive, the next, she was dying. I jumped back as blood sprayed everywhere. Kelsey's mouth worked open and shut, but no noise came out. She didn't have a larynx anymore. Anger flashed in her eyes followed by fear and then they grew dull, foggy with death. She wouldn't come back, not from that, the blood loss was too fast.

"I could've done that," I said. In fact, I'd wanted to. I'd been squeamish with Ronnie, but was angry enough at Kelsey to want to feel her flesh give and rip under my fingers.

He shook his head, wiping his hands on a rag someone handed him. "Pack justice is my job and it's better for you and Jackson both if I do this."

I nodded. Cal was probably right. The last thing Jackson needed was to watch his mate kill someone from his home pack.

Cal put an arm around my shoulder and turned me toward Jackson. I made to walk over to him, but Cal held me back. Bending down to my ear, he whispered, "Don't worry about your wolf. You're way too strong to be stunted now. Besides, I hear Jackson knows how to bring a wolf."

I laughed. "That he does." He let me go then and I rejoined Jackson, who wrapped me in his arms once again.

Cal motioned toward the wolves who'd been holding Kelsey. "Get her body ready to send back to her pack for burial." The men nodded and dragged her off.

Turning to face the rest of the pack, Cal said, "Okay. Show's over for now. Get back to your business, folks."

"Wait a minute," shouted someone. "What if she can't change?"

"You gotta shift to be in the pack," said someone else.

I shook my head. It was starting already. A growl rumbled in Jackson's chest, strong enough that it shuddered through my body, too. I patted his forearm. After Kelsey and the rogue, I didn't have it in me to worry about insular wolf politics. Not just then.

Cal held up his hands. "Calm down folks. It's been a long day. Let's give Chloe some time and see what happens. There's no rush."

"But it's pack law," protested a wolf named Joe. He was an older man and owned the gas station in town. "You gotta be a wolf to be pack."

Cal drew himself up to his full height. "Chloe saved us from a rogue alpha, that earns her a concession from me," he pointed to himself, "the pack alpha. Drop it unless you want to challenge me. I'll prove my blood on yours."

Joe licked his lips, nervous at the full brunt of Cal's authority, and shook his head. Cal stared at the crowd until they began to disperse, muttering and casting dark looks my way.

I flashed a sweet smile at them. "You're welcome. I was glad to do my duty by the pack, no matter the price I paid."

A few of the wolves ducked their heads in shame as I called them out.

I looked at Jackson. "The way I feel right now, I wouldn't cry if you didn't become alpha after Cal. Folks don't seem to appreciate what we do for them around here."

He nodded. "They're just scared. Give them some time. It's been a big day."

"Tell me about it." I wrapped my arms around his neck. "Take me home, Jacks."

16

On our way home, Jackson stopped at the gas station so I could wash the blood off my hands and scrub off the worst of the dirt. The girls would be wolves one day. They would know the taste of blood, the feel of a pulse under their teeth, but, until then, I felt the need to shelter them. They didn't need to see me covered in gore.

The second I stepped into the house, Mara and Sara greeted me with open joy, slamming into me with tight hugs.

I held them close. "Hey girls."

"Chloe, you're okay." Mara touched my hair as if she didn't quite believe I was real.

"We thought you went gone for good, that the rogue got you," Sara said with a sniff.

"I would never leave you girls." I kissed them both on the forehead. "I saw your parents by the way."

"You did?" Mara's eyes went wide.

"They helped me take down the rogue alpha. They're heroes."

"I wish they would come back," whispered Sara.

"Me too, sweetheart, but, until then, I promised I would take care of you."

"What about Grammy? She can't be alone. She needs us." Sara's brow furrowed with concern.

"Then I'll keep an eye on her too, but you girls aren't alone anymore. You have me."

"And me," said Jackson, his arms folding us into one big group hug. "Actually, I think you should both live here."

"Really?" asked Mara, her voice spiraling up into an excited squeal. Tears shone bright in both girls' eyes.

"That sounds like a great idea, doesn't it? Welcome home, girls." I gave them both a big squeeze. A lightness filled my heart, like helium in a balloon, the levity a welcome change in mood after the last few days. I released the girls after one last squeeze. "Now, let me go get cleaned up."

"I'll make pancakes while you take a shower," offered Jackson.

Sara clapped her hands with delight. "He makes the best pancakes, Miss Chloe."

"I bet he does." I felt a brief twinge of jealousy at being usurped in the pancake making department, but a more practical relief quickly came to the fore. If Jackson could cook, that meant I didn't have to. Plus, he washed dishes, too. I was a lucky woman.

In the shower, I closed my eyes and let the hot water cover me. My whole body ached. My wolf stared at me with golden eyes, silent and still. I tried to reach out to her, but couldn't make the connection. She was there, but we'd been separated by science I didn't understand. I didn't know how to make it right, either.

"Damn it," I said quietly, not wanting to be overheard. This was the last thing I needed. Being without my wolf would call everything into question no matter how strong I'd felt in that moment after I'd killed Ronnie. My place in the pack and my mate would be lost just because of one measly injection.

Hard as I tried to sniff them back, tears burned their way down my cheeks at the thought of going back to square one. I didn't want to be that girl again, the nobody to no one. Weak with fear, I leaned against the shower tile and let it hold me up.

A second later, Jackson poked his head into the bathroom. I quickly straightened up and made a show of washing my hair, hoping he wouldn't see or smell my distress.

"The pancakes are done, babe. You hungry?"

My stomach growled at the mention of food. It'd been a lifetime since I'd eaten. "I'll be right there." I tried to sound cheerful, but couldn't keep a small warble out of my voice.

If Jackson noticed, he didn't let on. Maybe he was giving me space. Maybe I'd earned a small breakdown.

"Don't take too long or the girls will eat your share." He shut the door and left me alone.

I quickly finished my shower, stubbornly refusing to cry anymore. I was strong, I reminded myself. Even if I never shifted again, I was no weakling. I'd done right by my pack and my mate. That would have to be enough. *That might be all you have*, said a small voice in my head, one I swiftly told to shut up.

Wearing a pair of yoga pants and one of Jackson's t-shirts, I padded, barefoot, out to the dining room and joined everyone at the table. They'd started eating without me, but I caught up in no time. Jackson really did make awesome pancakes. They practically melted on my tongue.

We passed the rest of the evening playing charades, purposely avoiding serious topics until the girls went to bed. I was grateful for the reprieve. I needed a break from all the drama. Once Mara and Sara were tucked in, Jackson poured us both a shot of whiskey and we snuggled on the couch.

"How are you doing?" He asked.

"I don't know, Jacks." I rested my head on his shoulder. "It's been a hell of a day. How are you?"

"Numb, I think." He kissed the top of my head. "I can't believe Kelsey would do that."

"I know."

"My pack will be so ashamed."

"They won't be mad that we killed her?" From what I understood, execution of wolves from other packs had to be approved by their home pack alpha first.

"No, not in this case. She'd made her bed, there's no

question she deserved to die."

"She was like a sister to you."

He snorted. "Apparently one I never really knew."

"I'm sorry." I threaded my fingers through his and gave a little squeeze.

"How's your wolf?"

I closed my eyes and we stared at each other. She seemed to be moving more freely now, but I couldn't feel her fur prickling under my skin or the rush of her trying to jump through. "I don't know." I gave a sharp almost panicked laugh. All my earlier 'I am woman, I am strong' resolve had begun to crumble in the face of my wolf's continued impairment. "In the end, Vicki may be right, I might end up an Omega. A wolf too weak to shift."

Jackson rocked me in his arms. "Sh. Don't say that. It'll be okay. You just need some time to rest and recover. You might be in shock."

"You think so?" I looked up at him and he kissed me.

"Yeah, I do." His hand gripped my hair tight against my scalp and he buried his nose in my neck. "Chloe. Oh God. Chloe." He almost sounded like he was crying. "I thought you were gone. I failed you. I didn't protect you. I ignored your instincts about Kelsey. Can you ever forgive me?" He let me go and slid off the couch to kneel in front of me, head bowed.

I pulled on his hands trying to get him to come back up next to me, but he was a dead weight. "Jacks, it's not your fault. You couldn't have known."

"You're my mate. If I can't keep you safe, I wouldn't blame you for walking away."

My jaw dropped. Yes, I had my doubts at our moving-at-the-speed-of-light mating, but the last thing I wanted was to be alone again. "You're my mate. No matter what. Nothing that's happened has changed that. I love you." I paused in shock then. I'd never said those words before.

"I love you, too." He returned to the couch and we resumed cuddling.

I rubbed his nose with mine. "Our first I love yous."

"Yeah."

We both smiled stupidly at each other and then Jackson leaned in for a kiss so deep, I thought he would swallow me whole.

Breaking our kiss, he stood and said, "Wait here. I have something I want to show you."

He disappeared into our bedroom and returned a second later, hands hidden behind his back.

I raised my eyebrows. "What is it?"

Jackson didn't answer, but came to kneel in front of me.

"Jackson? What's going on?"

"This." He showed me a fist and then opened it to reveal a black velvet box.

I touched the box, finger skimming the soft velvet. "Is that what I think it is?"

"Open it and see."

Taking the box, I opened it and gasped at the beautiful ring inside. A square cut diamond flanked by sapphires twinkled at me. "It's gorgeous."

He grinned. "You like it."

I nodded. "Very much."

"I ordered it weeks ago and it just arrived. It killed me not to tell you." He took the box from me, and clearing his throat said, "So, Chloe Weiss, will you marry me?"

All the doubts and worries from the last few weeks tumbled through my mind and I dismissed them one by one. Even if I never shifted again, I was wolf enough to be the alpha's mate. Our bond could not be broken and I wanted Jackson more than ever. I belonged at his side and no place else. Sniffing back tears, I said, "Yes."

He slipped the ring on my finger and we both looked at it for a moment.

"Wow," I said, turning my hand this way and that and watching the diamond catch the light. "I love it."

"It was always you, Chloe. You're my wolf, my love, my life." He moved to sit beside me on the couch again and gave me scorching kiss that seemed to sear my soul. His hands traced my curves through the t-shirt I wore.

He paused, lips lifting off mine to say, "Hey, is this my shirt?"

I nodded. Wanting to keep his scent close, I'd picked one of his shirts to wear. It made me feel safe, like I wasn't alone.

"I like it on you, but I like you even better without it." He lifted it off me and covered me himself, the heat of his chest burning into mine.

I stopped him then, thinking of the girls. "We should go to bed." I'd noticed the girls slept like their batteries had been removed, but on the off chance anyone woke up, I didn't want them to find us going at it like wererabbits. The last thing I needed after everything else, was to explain the birds-and-bees to kids who still believed in Santa.

Jackson didn't say anything, just scooped me up and carried me there. He set me gently on the bed.

"I won't break," I said.

"I know. You're not fragile, you're precious." He sank into bed beside me. "You're my heart, Clo. I can't live without you."

I swallowed hard as tears pricked my eyes. That was probably the sweetest thing anyone had ever said to me. "Jacks."

He put a finger to my lips. "Shh. Just let me love you."

"Forever." I sighed into his hand. I was home. I had a mate. It finally felt real.

To start, Jackson gave me a nice massage, using a scented oil that smelled of lavender and oranges. He rubbed the kinks out of my legs and the soreness out of my arms. Then he rolled me over and straddled my hips as he turned my back into putty. His hands touched me everywhere, imparting warmth, relaxation and, most of all, love. His feelings for me poured out through his fingers, a palpable thing that I soaked up with the massage oil.

"Oh, that feels so good," I moaned.

"That's what I'm aiming for." He flipped me back over and then sank to his knees at the end of the bed. His hands wrapped around each of my feet in turn.

I was a puddle by the time he started kissing his way up my legs. He parted my legs with a gentle hand. His fingers spread my inner lips wide, exposing the sensitive nub underneath. I didn't really pay much attention to his finger, being too lost in a massage induced coma, but when his tongue flicked over my core, my eyes flew open.

"Oh," I said.

He paused. "Oh, give me more or oh, stop?"

I gave a throaty laugh. "Give me more, naturally. When have I ever said stop?"

"There's always a first time." His tongue resumed its merciless circling around my core.

My breath came out in a gasp and my hips bounced up and down. "Well it won't be tonight."

I felt rather than saw the slow grin that split his lips. "Does that mean I can have my way with you?"

I spread my legs wider. "Please."

His head dipped down and his tongue worked me with the precision of a machine. My hips circled and danced under him. When he latched on and sucked as he worked the tip of his tongue back and forth across the very tip of my most sensitive spot, I lost it. With a soft cry, I came.

Jackson kept his tongue firmly in place no matter how

wildly I bucked. Slipping a few fingers into my wet passage, he pressed against other, more sensitive places hidden in my body. Before I knew it, a second orgasm chased the first, shuddering through me in a crashing tide.

After that, he gave me minute to recover. Climbing up my body, he kissed me, his tongue a mix of flavors, both his and mine. His scent filled my mind and I opened my mouth wider, wanting more of him than he'd already given.

He moved to kiss and nibble my neck with both hard and soft bites. Some would probably leave marks, but I didn't care. My breasts, he scooped up and slowly teased the nipples into stiff points with his tongue. Once they stood at attention, he bit them too, not hard enough to mark, but hard enough to make me gasp and for my stomach to tighten.

"Jacks," I moaned, my hands tracing his shoulders en route to bury themselves in his hair. "Oh, please."

"Please what, baby?"

"I need you."

"I'm going to give you everything you need and more." He clamped his teeth around a nipple and used his tongue to thrash the tip.

I writhed underneath him, feeling empty inside. "I want you, Jacks. Don't make me wait."

Being a gentleman, he obliged, slipping into me with one smooth thrust. My body quivered around him, and, for the first time, my wolf showed signs of real life. She howled and pranced.

Jacks wolf sauntered into my mind's eye, acknowledging her with a nod. She sank to the ground, rolling over in submission. He laid down next to her, pressing himself against her, giving comfort and reassurance. The whole thing gave me hope. One, that Jackson would stick with me no matter what, and two, my wolf might be okay.

I didn't have long to dwell on it though, because Jackson hauled my legs up and over his shoulders. Gone was the gentle regard he'd treated me with earlier. He took me with a wild roughness that made my blood run hot. I reached around to dig my hands into his thighs, urging him on. I wanted him harder and faster until we both exploded.

He howled softly when he came. I did too and our voices twined together, a harmony once lost but now found again. I felt a prickling rush under my skin too, which brought a smile to my face.

"What is it?" Jackson asked not missing the change in my expression.

"I can feel my wolf. She's coming back."

He let my legs drop back onto the bed and then collapsed on top of me, still buried in my slick wetness. "I knew she would."

I ran a hand through his hair. "I wasn't so sure."

"You doubt yourself too much, Clo. Your wolf may have come late but she's powerful." He kissed me. "Now go to sleep. It's been a long day."

We spooned and drew the covers in close to ward of the

increasing winter chill. I didn't sleep though. Instead I spent the night looking at my ring, feeling the heat of my mate at my back and keeping vigil over my wolf, waiting for her to regain full strength.

EPILOGUE

We had an old-fashioned wedding in August, full of wildflowers and happy sunshine in a bright blue sky. I'd been worried that Jackson's pack would think it low class, but it turned out no one shared Kelsey's tastes. They would've found chrome just as weird as I had.

His family welcomed me with open arms and apologized profusely for Kelsey. I had the sense they were worried I would blame them. Vicki stayed out of my way and was polite when she had to deal with me, which was more than I'd hoped for. Cal told me she was leaving, going out to visit some other packs in the hopes of finding a mate.

The rest of the Huntsville pack got over their reservations about me when I proved I could shift. It helped that Jackson and Cal both encouraged and supported me as I took on the alpha's mate role.

I started with Grammy, who we found unable to care for

herself let alone the kids. She hadn't been eating either. I assigned some of the pack to care for her. They didn't want to do it at first, but I was too alpha now for any wolf to say no to me. All I had to do was remind them about how I cut off a rogue alpha's head and that usually did the trick.

In a lot of people's memories, I was still that null who should've been run out of town, but things were changing for the better. Slowly. In a weird way, Kelsey may have done me a favor. Killing Ronnie had given me a lot of credibility.

Jackson and I kept Mara and Sara full-time, wanting them to have a stable home life. They were growing faster than I could keep up. It seemed every other week I had to run into town to buy more clothes. They'd been without proper nutrition for so long, no doubt their bodies had a lot of time to make up for. I also worked with them on reading and their grammar quickly showed signs of improvement. Given the right environment, they learned fast. I was proud of them.

We saw their parents here and there, still stuck in wolf form and showing no signs of shifting back. The girls accepted it as normal and didn't expect any different, but it would always tug at my heart. This was a 'death' I found difficult to accept. Their parents were alive, yet just as absent as my dead-and-buried mom and dad.

Being pregnant made it all worse, because I knew exactly how precious the life stirring in me was. Yep, I was knocked up when I walked down the aisle. Jackson was still a little surprised.

Honestly, though, what did he expect would happen? If you act like a wererabbit in heat, you multiply like one.

I couldn't wait to be a mom. Jackson was great with the girls and he was great with me; massaging my feet, bringing me ice cream, and generally treating me like a queen. I didn't know what the next chapter in our life held, but I knew this much; I had him, I had my wolf and I had a family to love.

Thank you for reading! Yes, this is where the story stops...for now. There's always something happening in Huntsville so I'm sure there will be more! If you enjoyed Jackson and Chloe's story please leave a review. It is a huge help and deeply appreciated.

Remember subscribers to my newsletter get a free novella (which was a bestseller when it was available for sale). My newsletter is also packed with cool giveaways, exclusive snippets and other fun. You can sign up by visiting www.authormfox.com (look for the newsletter in the right side bar!).

By the way, I also run The Wolf Pack, one of the largest and most amazing paranormal romance reader groups on Facebook. If you haven't joined the pack, you're missing out on free reads from all your favorite authors and lots of fun. You should come check us out! (Just search for us on Facebook, we'll pop right up!)

Other Books in the Huntsville Series

BRING HER WOLF

How the Huntsville series got its start!
Back in 2012 I wrote a short story about how Chloe and Jackson met that sold like crazy. It's now free with more than 100,000 downloads and 1000+ reviews across all retailers. So if you want to read what happened before The Alpha's Mate, just download Bring Her Wolf!

THE ALPHA'S JUSTICE
Huntsville Pack Book 2

5 fangs from Paranormal Romance Junkies!

He believes they're fated mates, but all she wants to do is kick him in the balls.

Gretchen Luna became a diehard Daddy's girl the day her mother ran out on them both. She doesn't believe in love and isn't looking for it, but when her ailing father is attacked and left bloody by wolves on the wrong side of the law, she goes out in search of what she does believe in: Justice.

Sheriff Talon Garde has way too much on his plate. Humans have breached shifters' carefully guarded privacy and are about to go public. If he can't stop them, what happened to Gretchen's father is going to be the least of everyone's worries.

More importantly, despite Talon's rep as a bad ass alpha whose growl strikes fear in the hearts of criminals, Gretchen's scent makes him go all squishy inside. She's THE ONE, he's sure of it. There's just that small matter of protecting the entire shifter species, saving her father and somehow convincing Gretchen it's pointless to fight fate…ideally while wearing a cup.

Standalone novel with NO cliffhanger.

THE ALPHA'S FIGHT
Huntsville Pack Book 3
When you've lost your wolf, how do you get it back?

'Jane Doe' has no idea who she is or why she wakes up in a…nursing home? Full of shifters? She may not be old, but they say she *is* a shifter—only her wolf is MIA and she's in some kind of trouble she can't remember to boot. And there's this guy, Ryder. Something about him that makes her tingle in all the right places. If only she knew whether or not she already had a mate, why she's been stashed in shifter 'retirementville' and where the hell her animal half went.

What if your wolf picked a mate you couldn't trust?

Former pro-fighter Ryder Chase plans to get away from his no-good pack alpha, Mason, and forge a new life for himself, but there's one little problem named Jane. Ryder's wolf wants her more than he wants to breathe. *Mate. Mine.* Finding his mate would be good news except for the part where she knows Mason. Is Jane mixed up with his alpha's dark side and everything Ryder wants to leave behind?

Full length, stand alone novel. No cliffhangers! Lots of plot!

For the love of fangs & fur

ABOUT THE AUTHOR

NY Times and USA Today Bestselling author Michelle Fox lives in the Midwest with her husband, kids, the occasional exchange student and the best dog ever. She loves fantasy and romance, which makes writing paranormal romance a natural fit. Occasionally, she goes through a maverick phase and writes contemporary romance. In her spare time, she's been known to shake her bon-bon at Zumba, make spectacular cheesecakes, hoard vintage costume jewelry and eat way too much ice cream (Ben and Jerry's Karamel Sutra for the win!).

Made in the USA
Las Vegas, NV
05 August 2021